**Winner of the Edgar Award—
Best Young Adult Mystery Novel**

CAREFUL WHAT YOU THINK
CAREFUL WHAT YOU ASK

"Daddy," Terri said. "I've been thinking about my mother. I don't know anything about her. I think you should tell me some things."

"Terri, that's the past. You're growing up, almost a young lady. You've got everything ahead of you. Why be morbid?"

Terri persisted. "My mother's name was Kathryn. That's all I know about her. And that she was killed in a car crash when I was four years old."

He didn't answer. His silence meant, I don't want to talk about this. She hesitated. Should she stop before she made a fool of herself? Or before they arrived at that point of stubborn silence where she would have to challenge him to get what she wanted? She had questions. She needed answers. She wanted answers. Only the worst part was, she didn't know exactly what it was she wanted—or what she might find out.

TAKING TERRI MUELLER

NORMA FOX MAZER

AN AVON FLARE BOOK

TAKING TERRI MUELLER is an original publication of Avon Books.

AVON BOOKS
A division of
The Hearst Corporation
1350 Avenue of the Americas
New York, New York 10019

Copyright © 1981 by Norma Fox Mazer
Published by arrangement with the author
Library of Congress Catalog Card Number: 81-65081
ISBN: 0-380-79004-1

First Avon Flare Printing: November 1981

AVON FLARE TRADEMARK REG. U.S. PAT. OFF. AND IN OTHER COUNTRIES, MARCA REGISTRADA, HECHO EN CANADA.

Printed in Canada

UNV 20

For Gloria Yerkovich and all the other parents
who are still waiting for
their children to return.

For as long as she could remember it had been the two of them. "Me and Daddy. Daddy and me." That was a song she sang when she was little. "Me and Daddy. Daddy and me. Oh how nice it be. Daddy and me." She sang herself to sleep at night. "Daddy and me, Daddy and me. Oh how nice it be."

Once there had been a mother, also. Terri, Daddy, and Mommy. She didn't remember. She had been four when her mother died. She didn't remember. That was funny. Not funny that made you laugh. The other funny. Sad funny. She didn't remember what her mother looked like, how she smelled, or if she was tall or short. Daddy talked to her about everything, but he didn't like to talk about her mother. It made him sad.

She knew what sad meant. Mostly she was happy. But sometimes she was sad. She didn't know why. It was silly to get sad. Daddy told her stories about Sally the Mouse who traveled with her father, Mustafa the Mouse, in their Mousemobile. Sally the Mouse was very smart, but sometimes she was sad, and sometimes she had a Bad Temper. But mostly she was a good little Sally the Mouse who made her father Happy and Proud.

Terri sat on her father's lap, her arms around his neck. Tell me a Sally the Mouse story.

7

Have you been a good girl?
Yes, yes, yes.
Did you learn a lot in school today?
Yes, yes, yes.
Were you an outstanding first-grade girl?
Yes, yes, yes.
Well, let's find out what Sally the Mouse has been up to.

Yes, she was a good girl. She was Daddy's good girl. They liked to travel and visit places. They had a car, a red Pinto. Her name was Terri Mueller. Daddy's name was Phil Mueller. Terri and Phil. Phil and Terri. Hurry, Terri. I will, Phil. You're a berry, Terri. You're a pill, Phil.

She loved the Pinto. She loved Daddy. They lived in lots of different places. "My, what a memory," her teacher said. "She learns so fast." Daddy was Proud.

Every year she had a birthday in April. Every year Daddy took her out to dinner on her birthday. They got all dressed up. He let her sip his wine and gave her nice presents. One year her present was Barkley. So you never have to be alone again, Daddy said, even when you're waiting for me to come home from work. Barkley hardly ever barked. She loved him very much.

She was eight years old . . . she was nine years old . . . she was ten years old. She and her father had fun together. He even made it fun when they cleaned house. Once, cleaning windows in a new apartment, he wrote messages on the windows with spray cleaner. "HELLO, TERRI. DO YOU LIKE THIS PLACE?" "THE MICE ARE HOLDING A CONVENTION UNDER THE SINK." His best message was written over the last three windows. "HELP! I CAN'T CONTROL MY URGES. STOP ME BEFORE I CLEAN MORE WINDOWS."

They had lived in so many places—big cities like New York and Chicago, and little towns like Hap Falls, Amberville, and Roarin. She could remember all the cities and towns, and all the different apartments, and all the people she had met.

She was eleven years old . . . twelve years old . . . thirteen years old . . . Her head was full of faces and places and names, but even when she tried very hard she still couldn't remember her mother.

One

"Terri, did you see the kitchen?" Phil Mueller's voice echoed off the walls of the empty room.

"I'll be there in a sec." Terri was checking out the bedroom that would be hers if they took this apartment. "Bed over here," she said, pacing around. "Bureau here?" And she imagined her posters tacked up, covering every inch of bare wall, including cracks and stains. She liked the long windows that faced on a little bit of a park across the street.

Her father came into the room. "Nice, very nice," he said, looking around. "Don't you think so?"

"How much is the rent?"

He shrugged. "Not cheap, but not a killer, either. We can go for it. Looks like a nice neighborhood, too."

"I could walk to school from here," she said. They had passed the junior high on the way from the rental agency. "But there's no garage, or side parking. Did you notice? That means parking the camper on the street."

"Camper's kind of big for street parking," Phil said.

"It's not *that* busy a street," Terri said. "If we still had our Pinto it wouldn't matter so much."

Phil groaned. "You'll never stop talking about the Pinto, will you, Terri?"

"It was my sweet little car." Right up until last year they'd had the Pinto with the stick shift. Red Ryder,

10

her father called it. Whenever they drove at night Terri would climb over the front seat and curl up in back to sleep. Barkley was always very alert and excited in the car and would sit by the back window watching everything and taking up more than his share of space. But even though she had to really scrunch up, Terri never minded and always slept in the car just as well as she did in her own bed.

In fact, since they'd had so many apartments, but only one Pinto, she had thought of *that* almost as her real home. Speeding along the highways between cities and states, she and her father chewed over where they'd been living and where they'd live next, what kind of place they'd look for, and the interesting people they were sure to meet.

Often, when they traveled, they ate out in diners and restaurants, but just as often they'd shop in a supermarket and buy special things to eat in the car like Lorna Doones and bunches of green grapes. Their favorite traveling food, though, was always a plain old bread, bologna, cheese, and lettuce sandwich.

They didn't have too many rules in their life because Phil said—and Terri agreed—that the main rule was to be thoughtful about each other. That covered a lot of territory, such as each of them letting the other know where they were at all times, and not waiting for the other person to clean up any messes Barkley made. In the car, though, they did have rules, such as no eating peanuts in the shell (too messy), and no soft drinks (Phil didn't approve of the caffeine), and no driving while sleeping. That was Terri's rule for Phil, because she wasn't old enough yet to share the driving.

Once she had asked him how he decided where they'd move to next. "Well, I don't really decide, Terri," he'd said. "We just get in the car and go, until it feels like it's time to stop. When something clicks—I trust that. I trust my instincts and feelings. You know how it is."

But, in fact, she didn't know, didn't really under-

11

stand that sense of being carried along by instinct. She began to think of her father as emotional and herself as rational and sensible.

She was a tall girl with long hair that she sometimes wore in a single braid down her back, and sometimes parted in the middle with a wing of hair pulled back and held with a barrette on either side of her face. She was quiet and watchful and didn't talk a lot, although she *liked* to talk, especially to her father, with whom she felt she could talk about anything. They were close, very close, companionable, and easy with each other, and she sometimes thought of him as her real best friend, distinct from the best friends she made in whatever school she happened to be attending.

He had taught her to drive in the Pinto when she was eleven years old. On Sunday afternoons in a deserted parking lot, she'd practice J turns, parking, and stopping on a dime. Her father would laugh and say, "Terri, you'll have your driver's license before you have your learner's permit."

She had always thought she'd take her driver's test in the Pinto, but last year on her twelfth birthday, they traded in the Pinto for the camper truck. She had hated to see the Pinto go and shed real tears for it, as many, in fact, as for the various mice, hamsters, and guinea pigs who had come and gone in her life.

But quite soon she became devoted to the camper and hoped they would never trade it in. The cab was like an ordinary pickup truck, but in back a little metal house sat on the truck bed. Inside were two beds, a sink, propane refrigerator and stove, table and benches, and a minute bathroom with a chemical toilet. Everything was small and every bit of space was used. There was a water tank underneath and a metal luggage rack on top.

"The camper makes us completely free," Phil said when they bought it. "Anytime we get the urge to travel, we can just go, Terri. And stop wherever we want to."

They rarely stayed in any place for more than six or eight months. Terri had heard her father say, "I've got restless feet," so many times that she almost thought of his feet as having a life of their own, as if it were Mr. Restless Feet, and not Mr. Philip Mueller, who kept them on the move.

Last year, for instance, Terri had gone to school in Richmond, Indiana, until June when they went south to Wilmington, North Carolina. In August they drove north again and decided to live in Niagara Falls, mostly because they both got hooked on the awesome Falls. Then in June, after school was over, they drove to where they were now, Ann Arbor, Michigan.

Wherever they landed, Phil had little trouble finding work. He was a carpenter and an all-around Mr. Fixit. "I wouldn't be without you, Terri," he told her, "and I wouldn't be without my toolbox."

The toolbox, a large green metal box, with double handles, about the size of a bureau drawer, was always with them, even if they went out for a short Sunday drive. It probably weighed a hundred pounds full. It used to be that Terri couldn't budge it—she would try regularly—but now, using both hands, she could just lift it and stagger a step or two.

The tools—the hammers, wrenches, pliers, the do-all, wood chisels, levels, planes, and saws—were as familiar to her as her own face. That, and her father's wide leather nail belt with its pockets and dangling hammer slings that he wore when he was working, slung low around his hips like a cowboy.

Down in Wilmington, Mrs. Lawrence, who ran the Bide-A-Wile Trailer Park, where they had stayed for the summer, had hired Terri to take care of her kids, Meg and Nate. At the end of the day they'd all sit outside on the Lawrences' trailer stoop and wait for Phil Mueller to come home.

"My," Mrs. Lawrence said nearly every day, "he *is* very good looking."

And remembering that now, Terri asked slyly, "Daddy? You recall Mrs. Lawrence?"

"Who?" He was hunkered down, checking the radiator.

"Mrs. Lawrence from the Bide-A-Wile Trailer Park."

"Oh, *Fran*. Sure." He looked over his shoulder at Terri. "What about her?"

"You know what she used to say about you?"

"It must be funny from that look on your face."

Terri folded her arms in imitation of the trailer park manager. " 'My,' " she drawled, " 'he *is* very good looking.' "

Her father laughed. "Is that what she said? Never told me that."

"What did she say when you went out on dates?"

"Dates?" Phil pulled a face. "You make me sound like your teenaged father."

"They were dates," Terri said. "You went to the movies with her, didn't you? Did you buy her popcorn? What else did you do?"

"Subject closed."

She would have teased him a little more, but just then a woman walked into the empty apartment. "Oh!" She stared in surprise. "Excuse me, I didn't know anyone else was here." Her hair was tucked into a red bandanna. She was holding a little boy by the hand. "Are you looking at this apartment, too?"

"We'll be through in a few minutes," Phil said.

"Don't rush on my account. It's just—they didn't tell me in the rental office." She opened the bathroom door. "Is this real tile? How neat! Most places have everything fake these days."

The little boy was wearing blue and white striped overalls that said Oshkosh B'Gosh. He had big brown eyes and light frothy hair. "Hi," Terri said. He got behind his mother, then peeked out with a serious expression.

14

"Say hi to the girl, Leif," his mother said. "Say hi, honey."

He shook his head.

"That's okay," Terri said.

"This really is a neat place," the woman said. "What fantastic windows."

Terri liked that she didn't badger the child to say hi. She really hated it when adults did that to kids. She'd noticed that a lot of adults thought kids had no private life, that they could say or do anything to children just because they were bigger.

"It's a fine apartment," her father said to the woman.

"If you only knew some of the dumps I've been looking at. Am I sorry you're here first!" She had big excited eyes and a big grin. "I'm going to take a look at the kitchen—just in case you guys decide not to take this place." She held up crossed fingers.

Terri and her father finished inspecting the apartment. "So, what do you think?" Phil asked. "It won't be easy to heat with those big windows."

"Yes, but the living room—" There was a real working brick fireplace, and Terri already had visions of them playing checkers and eating popcorn in front of a crackling blaze. "I think we should take it," she said.

"Okay," her father said. "Let's."

Just then the child and his mother came into the room. "Don't you love that fireplace?" She said, "Luu-uuuuve," and her eyes got even bigger. "I bet you're taking this apartment."

"Well . . . we're discussing it," Phil said.

Discussing it? Terri thought they'd just made their decision.

"We're probably not going to take it," he went on.

Well, there goes the fireplace, Terri thought. Seeing her father give her a wink, she said, "We think it would be hard to heat because of the windows."

"Oh, poo!" The woman waved her hands. "You can always wear another sweater. But can you always get a place right by a park, with a fireplace, and *elegant* windows?" She clapped her hand to her forehead. "What am I doing? Selling the place to you. Shut up, Nancy! Are you really turning it down? You aren't desperate—?"

"We're camping out right now," Phil said.

"That's wonderful! We're staying in a motel, and it costs a fortune. If I ever get my life in order I'm taking Leif camping. I really think it's a must-have experience for every child. Don't you?" She appealed to Terri.

Terri, not happy to be classified as a child along with the little boy, only smiled faintly.

Her father put his hand on her shoulder. "Terr— what do you say we let this lady have the apartment?"

"Look," the woman said, "you're not just being *nice*—?"

Yes, he is, Terri thought.

Her father leaned against the wall, arms folded across his chest. "Terri and I are old hands at this apartment hunting game. We'll probably have another place by tonight."

"Are you sure? Are you absolutely sure?" She looked from one to the other, then grabbed their hands. "It must be a good omen meeting such terrific people on my first week here. I came here to go to college and— Oh, excuse me! My name is Nancy Briet."

"Phil Mueller. And this is my daughter, Terri."

Nancy Briet shook Phil's hand, then Terri's. "And this is Leif, as you already know." She put her hand on her son's head. "Phil . . . Terri . . . Can I call you that?" Her smile was brilliant. "As soon as I'm settled, I'm inviting you to dinner."

"We'll hold you to that," Phil Mueller said.

Everywhere they went, there were women who liked her father, and women her father liked. Terri mostly understood. *If only,* she sometimes thought, as she thought now, leaving the apartment, *If only my mother . . .* She pushed the useless thought away and considered Nancy Briet. Friendly, warm, but not gushy. Blonde,

16

but not glamour blonde: underneath the red scarf, her hair had been loose and tangled. She liked her son and had mostly included Terri in the conversation. Points for Nancy Briet.

Would they see her again? Terri glanced at her father as he unlocked the truck. He was whistling between his teeth. In the cab she put her arms around Barkley, who had waited patiently for them, and remembered her small self listening gravely to her father's stories about Sally the Mouse who sometimes had a Bad Temper whenever her father, Mustafa the Mouse, wanted to do anything without her. Silly Sally didn't understand that Mustafa also needed friends his own age. Didn't she know that in the end they two would always go off together in their Mousemobile? And that would be that!

Two

It was always fun settling into a new place. Out of the U-Haul (or in this case, storage) came their dear familiar things: Terri's bed and bureau, their wooden-legged kitchen table with the cocoa-brown enameled top bordered with prancing horses, their TV and radios, her father's special chair, and the old beat-up red couch they kept meaning to replace.

On Denver Street they found a second-floor apartment, not as nice as the place with the long windows, but it was mid-August already, time to settle down, and it would certainly do very well. The phone company promised service in two weeks; Barkley and Terri did their usual explorations, locating the nearest market and gas station, and all the little shops and stores. Phil, who had a new job trussing roofs, said, "Terri, are you going to need clothes for school?" He peeled off bills from the rubber-banded roll he kept in his back pocket.

Terri yawned. "Maybe I'll do some shopping today."

"You better go back to bed first," her father said. "No use you getting up so early."

Terri poked at her boiled egg. If she didn't see her father at breakfast, it would be hours before she got to really talk to anyone. "Hi's" and hellos to salespeople didn't count. She'd be glad when school started.

"Don't forget to buy meat for tonight," Phil said, before he left.

"I won't. Hey! Your lunch." She handed him the lunch pail and thermos. He kissed the top of her head and left.

Later, after straightening up and making a vanilla cake for supper, she went out. She liked the new neighborhood. She didn't see many kids her age around, but there was a little movie theater that was almost like a doll's house, and up a hill behind an old abandoned church, there was a field overgrown with wild flowers and thorn apple trees: a perfect place for Barkley to run around and enjoy himself without bothering anyone else.

The days were draggy without school. Camping had been better. More kids around, and swimming to help pass the time. They were pretty well settled into the apartment. She had her room almost all fixed up. Windows looked down over a spare backyard and there was almost enough space on the walls for all her posters. "Up you go again," she said, tacking up her favorite of the girl and the farmhouse.

Most of the posters were of animals and, maybe because they'd never had a house of their own, about ninety percent of them had a house somewhere in the picture. Terri's favorite was a painting of a girl lying in a field of yellow grass with a book next to her, but not reading, just lying there on her stomach, her feet up, her chin in her hands. She was wearing a light blue dress the same color as the sky, and you could tell a wind was blowing from the way the grass bent. Far away behind the girl was an old silver-grey farmhouse. It was the sort of house, Terri thought, where they would have lots of old, nice, worn-out furniture, and tons of plants, and where a whole family lived—children, father, and a mother, too.

"Did we ever live on a farm?" she asked her father that night.

"A farm? Where'd you get that idea?"

Well, she didn't know, maybe just from dreaming

19

about the old silver farmhouse. "I thought maybe we did, with my mother."

"Nope," he said, and his face went blank. She called it his shut-the-door look. It always scared her a little. She wanted to see him smile again, so when he shut the door she didn't kick it open, just rapped a little, a light knock.

"I think I'll buy some goldfish," she said. Tap . . . tap . . . are you there? "I saw some really cute ones in the pet shop." She cleared the plates, tossed him a sponge to wipe the table.

"Goldfish," he said. His face relaxed, his lips curved up into a smile. "They're so dumb, Terr." He made fish noises with his mouth. "Hey, I think they're even dumber than guinea pigs." And as if the subject was finished, he said, "That was terrific cake. I'll take some to work tomorrow."

She ran hot water into the sink, poured in detergent. "My guinea pigs weren't dumb."

"No? Wheeek! Wheeek! Wheeek!"

"Daddy!" A few years before, all she had wanted for her birthday were guinea pigs. Phil had bought her two females—that's what they told him in the pet store—but pretty soon she had six guinea pigs and in a few weeks it became apparent she was going to have even more guinea pigs. They were pretty, every one a different combination of colors, but all they said was, "Wheeek! Wheeek! Wheeek!" Phil could hardly stand it. Finally Terri decided to sell them back to the pet shop. They *weren't* very interesting pets, but she'd always felt bad, disloyal really, that she got rid of them. It wasn't their fault they were dull.

"Anyway, they were beautiful," she said.

"Yeah, beautiful and dumb," Phil teased. "And goldfish are even *worse*. They don't have the brains to know their own mother, Terr."

She didn't know what touched her off. Maybe she was tired and didn't want to be teased. Maybe thinking about school starting soon was getting to her. She was going into junior high—a definite difference from elementary school. Or, maybe it was none of those things. She didn't get mad too often at her father. But suddenly she shouted at him. "You always want things your own way. You don't want me to buy goldfish because it's *my* idea!"

Hearing her, Barkley whined in a squeaky voice, as if he were a toy poodle instead of a big mutt.

"Barkley, quit that whining," her father said. "What's the matter, Terr?" He looked absolutely amazed.

"Nothing!" How could she tell him when she didn't know herself? "I'm going for a walk!" She had learned this from him. There were moments when he, too, had to "go for a walk," and by himself. She went up to the field and sat in the grass, and then lay down and watched clouds. She became calmer and felt as if someone were saying to her, It'll be all right, Terri.

When she came back her father was outside fixing a window on the camper. "See anything interesting?"

"Man on a pink horse," she said, still a little snappy.

"Did you see the sky?" He pointed. The sun was setting, huge, fiery red, with a band of pure green just above it. A strange sunset.

"It's a sun show," Phil said. "The greatest art on earth! Did you ever see anything like that?"

"Only about a thousand times."

He rolled his eyes. "Thirteen, and already a full-fledged skeptic." He put his arm around her waist. "You go ahead, get those goldfish—"

"No, I don't want them."

"A couple goldfish would be nice. They'd swim round and round all day, round and round and round and—"

"All right, all right." She had to laugh.

A few days later, while she was fixing lunch, the phone rang. She was surprised. It had been installed only the day before. "I bet it's Daddy," she said to Barkley, picking up the receiver.

21

"Hello—Terri?" a woman said. "This is Nancy Briet. Remember me?"

"Sure. Hi, how'd you get our phone number?"

"Your father called me this morning."

"He did?"

"Oh, sure, we've had quite a few nice little conversations these past couple weeks." That was news to Terri. "Listen, I want you two to come to dinner. I promised, remember!"

"How's Leif?" Terri said.

"Oh, super! I'm getting him enrolled in day care for the fall when I go back to school. Oh, boy, am I scared about that!" She gave a big laugh. "Listen, your father said check with you on a good day for dinner. How about Friday night?"

"Okay," Terri said.

"Come hungry. I'm going to cook up a storm."

The Friday dinner went so well that on Sunday, Phil, Terri, Nancy, and Leif all drove out to a county park for a picnic. While Phil and Terri worked on the fire, Nancy played with Leif. "My leafy Leif, my little tree."

"Not a tree."

"Oh, excuse me! You're a branch."

"Not a branch!"

"A twig?"

"No!"

She picked him up and held his face to hers. "I know, you're just my Leif."

"You look like Madonna and Child," Phil said.

"We do?" Nancy looked pleased.

"Madonna in blue jeans," Terri said, "and Child with mud on his nose."

"Oh, Terri, you know how to help a woman keep her feet on the ground," Nancy said. Later she was surprised to find out Terri's age. "I thought sure, fourteen or fifteen."

"What's the difference?" Phil said.

"Oh, a lot, Phil. A year at that age—? A *lot*."

"You only thought I was older because I'm tall," Terri said. She was almost always the tallest girl in her class.

"No, that isn't really it." Nancy turned to Phil. "There's something about your daughter—I would call her very poised. She knows how to be around grown-ups, don't you agree?"

Terri wished they'd drop the subject. Maybe she appeared poised to Nancy, but what she felt was embarrassed to be talked about in that confidential way, as if she weren't present.

"Let me tell you," Nancy said, "I've had girls Terri's age babysitting Leif, and oh boy, they can be real little pains. Just so self-absorbed."

"Want to play, Leif?" Terri turned her back, but of course she could still hear Nancy and her father.

"That's a very, very nice kid you've got there, Mr. Mueller."

"I like her."

"Well, I do, too!" Nancy said, but from the way she had been looking at Phil, Terri thought it was *him* she really liked. He did look very handsome and full of fun that day in Levi's, sneakers, and a Mickey Mouse tee shirt that said, Don't Mouse With Me.

At first, Terri wasn't sure how much she liked Nancy. Nancy talked fast and loud and sometimes swooped Leif up into her arms as if he were a pillow or a stuffed toy, holding him around the waist, his legs dangling. Leif didn't seem to mind, laughing and pounding on his mother until she noticed and straightened him up.

Again on the following Friday, the four of them ate supper together at Nancy's place. Phil brought a bottle of wine and Nancy had a fire going in the fireplace, although it was a warm evening. Nancy and her father got into an argument later—not much of one, but Nancy didn't back down. "I don't understand the way you two live," she said. "So you have a bed and a couch and two spoons and three plates. Don't you *want* things?"

"We have each other," Phil said.

"That's all very nice. I have Leif and he has me. I still feel the need for my own stuff—you know, it gives you a sense of *home,* no matter where you are. Don't you think so, Terri?"

"I like the way we live," she said. Did Nancy think she wouldn't defend her father? She wouldn't have said for the world that Nancy's argument had touched something in her, some longing that wasn't satisfied.

Nancy went on arguing and Terri said she'd read Leif a story and put him to sleep. But he wanted to play jumping games. "Okay, we'll play Hot Lava," she said, making it up as she went along. The whole game was this: Leif perched on his bureau, arms outstretched. Terri cried, "Hot Lava! Hot Lava all around, Leif! Leap for your life!" Then he jumped, she caught him, they hugged and kissed, he was safe, and they started all over again.

She turned around to see Nancy standing in the doorway watching. "I can see him in twenty years. He'll be walking up the aisle with his bride and whispering in her ear, 'Hey, I know this *neat* game.' "

"One more," Leif said. Terri put him up on the bureau. Funny, but she liked the game almost as much as he did. There was something so satisfying in catching him, feeling his arms go around her neck, and then holding him close for a moment. It was a feeling as if she really *had* saved him from some great danger.

One night, not too long after school had started, her father said, "Terr? Do you like Nancy?" It was a hot, still night, and all the windows were wide open. Terri was lying on the floor in shorts and tee shirt with her English book propped open on her stomach. She was reading a play about Nathan Hale, but thinking about Shaundra Smith, a girl in her gym class.

"I like Nancy," she said.

"She likes you." He was wearing cutoffs, his bare hairy legs swinging over the arm of the old red couch.

"Interesting, isn't it," he said, "how she's alone with her son, and I'm alone with you."

"But she has a lot of relatives," Terri said. Nancy had a sister in Ohio, a brother in New Orleans, parents in Florida, and as she said, "countless relatives everywhere else in the world." Another difference was that while Terri's mother had died in a car crash, Leif's father had walked out on him even before he was born.

"Do you like Nancy enough to, ah, for her to—" Her father, with an odd little smile on his face, cleared his throat, and Terri realized what he was going to say.

"You want to marry Nancy?" she blurted. They had always teased and joked about the ladies who liked him, and would this one or that one make her a good stepmother.

He looked relieved. "You really get down to the nitty gritty, daughter. The answer to your question is, Maybe. And if so, not right this instant."

"But you're thinking about it?"

"Let's just say I'm checking in with you on the idea. Nothing definite, nothing but an idea . . ."

"Okay, swell." She felt a rush of emotion and bewilderment. Daddy and her living with other people? She'd have to get used to that. They wouldn't just go moving around, would they, if he got married? Where would they live? Would she have to call Nancy "Mother"?

"Hey—" Her father nudged her leg with his bare foot. "I'm not doing anything in a rush. And I'm not doing anything you're not going to agree to. Nothing is changing today, or tomorrow, or for a long time."

"Okay," she said. She picked up her English book again, but she wasn't concentrating. "It would be nice to have a real family," she said after a while.

He was sipping a cold beer. "Oh, we're not real?"

"No, I mean—you know. Parents. Two. Like other people."

He held the beer can to his cheek. "Give me a break,

honey. Must be plenty of other kids have only one parent."

"Yes, but—" She shook her head, felt suddenly tight, and wanted to end the conversation. He was right—there were always kids around who were living with just one parent, and sometimes a kid whose mother or father had died. But all the same, it was never the same. Terri didn't know why, only that in some mysterious way she wasn't like other kids.

At the door Barkley moaned his take-me-out sound. Her father got the leash. Terri sat up. "Daddy? I've been thinking about my mother, and— Daddy, I don't know anything about her." He snapped the clip on the leash. "I think you should tell me some things."

"Terri, that's the past." He straightened up, held Barkley on a short leash. "You're growing up, almost a young lady . . . and you're beautiful. You've got everything ahead of you. Why be morbid?"

"I want . . . I just want . . ." Her voice fell away. She felt confused, then resentful. Why was it so bad to want to know about her mother?

"Bringing up things like this will only make us both unhappy."

She persisted. "My mother's name was Kathryn. That's all I know about her. And that she was killed in a car crash when I was four years old."

He didn't answer. They looked at each other over Barkley. His silence meant, I don't want to talk about this. She felt an answering stubbornness rising in her. He left with the dog, and she went to the window, looked down at the street, and watched the two of them walking toward the corner. She put her head out the opened window, feeling the impulse to yell, "You better tell me!" But that was childish. She wasn't a child anymore. She had questions, wanted to know things about her life. She needed answers. She wanted answers. She felt something strong in herself and said out loud, *"I want answers."*

26

\Three

"Shaundra, hi, Shaundra," Terri said, trying to sound casual. She looked up from tying her sneaker, which she had been tying for at least five minutes, as she waited on the corner near school for Shaundra Smith to pass. The old shoelace trick. If she and Shaundra got to be friends, maybe she'd tell her.

"Hi, Terri," Shaundra said, and she stopped. Great!

Terri picked up her books. Then, across the street she saw George Torrance, and for a moment she couldn't say anything. Was it a good luck sign, seeing George the first time she got to talk to Shaundra outside school?

"Where're you going?" Shaundra said.

"No place special. Home, I guess." Had George seen her? A few days before she had noticed him playing the oboe in band during an assembly. A skinny boy with glasses, but something about playing the oboe transformed him. She'd been sitting in the front row and couldn't get her eyes off him. Since then, everywhere she turned, she saw him.

"What'd you think of assembly?" Shaundra asked. For a moment Terri thought the other girl had read her mind. Then she realized Shaundra meant today's assembly. "Wasn't it gross?"

A man from the DA's office had talked to them on juveniles and the law in Michigan. Forty-five minutes of legal language.

27

"He was the most boring person I ever heard," Shaundra went on. She was a chubby girl with masses of dark, coarse hair hanging down like curtains around her face. She had a round face and round, dark eyes. "I think Mr. Hemphill was snoring," she said. "I know *I* was totally vegged out."

"He was boring, but I felt sorry for him," Terri said. The two girls walked along together.

"I didn't. He should have arrested himself for disturbing the peace!"

"I guess I just, in general, feel sorry for people like that. I mean, I wonder if they know they're boring everyone."

Shaundra pushed her hair off her face. "Even if they knew they wouldn't care. That's what makes them so boring."

"Want to go have a soda?" Terri said.

"Not a *Coke*. They rot your insides."

"I know, and they have a lot of caffeine, too. Only, did you ever have one with ice cream, milk, and vanilla flavoring?"

"Gross."

"No, it's good. My father and I make it sometimes."

"Popcorn is what I love. Popcorn and garlic."

"Garlic?"

"I know, isn't that disgusting? What'd you do this weekend?"

"Well, yesterday Nancy and Leif came over for breakfast. My father made blueberry pancakes. And on Saturday, I went shopping and bought this." She touched the short, plum-colored jacket she was wearing.

"How neat! Do you get a clothing allowance, or am I being too nosy?"

"My father gives me money for clothes and I buy what I want."

"Just like *that?*" Shaundra snapped her fingers. "Do you get a regular allowance?"

"Yes."

"Can you do anything you want with it?" Terri

28

nodded. "Do you pay for your own movies and records and things like that?"

"Sometimes, and sometimes my father pays."

"You're lucky. My mother makes me pay for everything. Even if I want some little makeup junk, or a pair of socks, if she doesn't think I *totally* need them, I have to earn the money."

"Well, I work," Terri said, a little defensively. She told Shaundra about the summer she took care of Meg and Nate. She liked working, but one of the problems with moving around was that by the time someone got to know you and trust you, it was just about when you were ready to move on. "Anyway, Daddy says I earn my allowance by the work I do in the house for us," Terri said.

"Like what? Do you mind this third degree?"

Terri smiled and shook her head. She thought it was a good sign when someone you wanted to be friends with wanted to know all about you. "I do cleaning, and fix suppers—things like that."

"Is there anything you have to do that you *hate?* Like cleaning bathrooms?"

"If I really hated it, I think Daddy would say, 'Okay, do something else.' He's not real strict about stuff like that."

"What is he real strict about?"

"That I let him know where I am and when I'm coming home—"

Shaundra rolled her eyes. "Tough life. Anything else?"

"Taking care of Barkley, things like defleaing him. Daddy says having an animal is like having a child. If you're not going to take care of it—forget it."

"You sure talk a lot about your father!"

"Well—my mother's, ah, dead." Terri's face got warm. Talking about her mother always embarrassed her.

Shaundra linked arms with Terri. "That's sad. I'm sorry. Who's Nancy? Your sister?"

29

"No, it's only me and my father. She's my father's girlfriend, and Leif is her little boy."

"What does she do?"

"Work, you mean? Something part-time with computers, and she's gone back to college to get her degree."

"What about your father? Aren't I nosy?"

"I don't mind. I like to know about people, too. Sometimes I wish I could look right into every house and see how people live. My father's a carpenter. What about your father?"

"He's a policeman, a detective, and my mother is a substitute teacher."

"A detective?" Terri said. "That's interesting." But it made her feel uncomfortable to imagine Shaundra's father putting handcuffs on someone and leading him away. She had seen a man like that on TV, his head hanging way down.

"I was in Detroit over the weekend visiting my father," Shaundra said. "He moved there after my parents got divorced. Now he's remarried. Don't you think parents are gross? Always thinking of themselves! 'Oh, Shaundra, you wouldn't want us to live together and just fight all the time!' That's what they said when they told me and my brothers they were splitting. You know what I said, Terri? I said, 'You can fight as much as you like. I don't care!' 'Well, we care,' they said. They pretended they were thinking about us, but they did it for themselves. Oh, *no*, don't let me get going on that!"

"Did you have a good time visiting?"

"Semi-good. My father spent at least fifty percent of the time complaining about my mother. I told him, 'She spends fifty percent of her time complaining about you!' They are so *dumb*, really. I hate it that they do that. At least, my stepmother doesn't say anything about her old husband."

"Is she nice?" Terri asked, thinking about Nancy.

"Francine's all right, at least she leaves me alone. We went to two movies and ate at this restaurant,

30

Captain Noah's. Francine said it was the best fish place in Detroit. Now how does she know that? There was a swordfish over the entrance, looked like he was going to fall right on you. Inside they had dead stuffed fish on the walls staring at you with their fishy eyes. I told Francine, 'Gee, what a wonderful way to improve people's appetites.' "

"When will you see your father again?" Terri asked, laughing.

"Maybe in two weeks."

"You must miss him!"

"I wouldn't mind seeing my mother every other week, either. That would be great. She drives me bananas. Well, semi-bananas."

"Well, here's my corner," Terri said. Was it too soon to ask Shaundra to come to her house? She wasn't sure yet if Shaundra wanted to be friends, or was just being friendly. There was a big difference.

"Okay. See you tomorrow then," Shaundra said.

"Right. See you in gym. Bye."

"Bye."

Terri walked away. In a moment she glanced back. Shaundra was looking back, too. "Bye!" they called, almost in unison.

Four

"When's that bell going to ring?" Shaundra muttered, jumping around and waving her arms in front of Terri.

"Come on, girls, spruce it up," Karen Trimbley, their gym teacher, yelled. "Shaundra, don't let Terri get away with that!"

The bell rang. Shaundra linked arms with Terri as they went into the locker room. "Want to come over to my house after school?"

"Okay." She didn't let herself sound excited or too glad. Not yet. Not till she was sure.

"Did I tell you my stepmother is going to have a baby?" Shaundra said later, as they turned down Logan Street.

"That's wonderful."

"You think so, Terri? We don't need any more kids in this family. I actually think they're semi-nuts to do it. My father's always complaining about supporting me and my brothers. That's three. And there's Francine's kids, my stepbrothers. Makes five. And now another kid?"

"Four brothers," Terri said. "I'm impressed."

"Well, don't be. I didn't give birth to them."

"Maybe your stepmother will have a girl—"

"A sister would be nice. Well, semi-nice."

Terri liked Shaundra's house a lot. There was a basketball hoop in the driveway and bushes in the yard. Inside, everything looked old and comfortable. In the living room the top of the piano was covered with framed pictures. "Who plays?" Terri asked.

"My mother, a little. She wants me to take lessons, but I have a tin ear."

"Can I look around?"

"Help yourself, but there's nothing to see."

Terri peeked into the bedrooms, noticing the rugs on the floors and spreads on the beds. Not to mention curtains at the windows.

"See that rocker?" Shaundra said, as they looked into her brothers' room. "That was my grandfather's. My mother lets my stupid little brothers have it. I can't believe it. They don't even care that it was Grandpa Morris's."

In the kitchen they made banana shakes, then took them into Shaundra's room. She had an old-fashioned four poster with fruit carved into each wooden post. "Was the bed your grandmother's?" Terri asked.

"Don't I wish! My mother bought it at a garage sale." Shaundra sat cross-legged on the bed. "All night, I feel like I have the ghosts of all the people who used to sleep in this bed, in bed with *me.*"

Terri laughed. She felt good being with Shaundra. "Who's this?" She pointed to one of the pictures tucked into the frame of the mirror.

"My grandparents Smith. My grandmother's sort of a sweet old boring type, but my grandfather thinks she's the greatest. Are your grandparents like that?"

"Well . . . no." This was the worst part of making new friends, having to keep saying it was only her and her father, and nobody else, except Aunt Vivian who they only saw once a year. "Is this you?" she said, pointing to another picture. "Who's with you?"

"Me and my mother." The picture showed the two of them seated with their backs to the piano, both looking straight into the camera, both with their hands clasped over their knees. Shaundra wore a dark turtleneck under a white shirt with the sleeves rolled up. Her mother was dressed almost exactly the same. They really looked alike. Her mother had even more hair than Shaundra, and wore it the same way, parted in the middle and hanging down on each side of her face.

Terri couldn't take her eyes off the picture. She had wondered for some time now if she looked at all like her mother. She and her father were both dark-haired, and they both had a small blotchy birthmark, like an amoeba, on their right shoulder, but otherwise—no, they really didn't look alike.

If only she had a picture of her mother. Not that it would make a difference, but she would *feel* different. It would be so nice to think—no, to *know,* and be able to say, "My hair is just like my mother's!" Or, "I have my *mother's* eyes."

"This is my cousin Basil," Shaundra said, pointing to another snapshot. Five people sitting on folding wooden chairs set up on a sidewalk, with five more people standing behind them. "This is my Uncle Norm, here's my Aunt Trudy, she's a sweetie pie, Uncle Julius, Aunt Connie, *so* nice . . . See *him,* that's Wendell, their son, he's a little retarded."

Terri tried to imagine having so much family, so many relatives, and all different. Some just babies, some old, one retarded, but yet all of them part of you. Maybe, she thought, it would be like going to a banquet, seeing a huge table covered with so many bowls of food you knew you could never eat it all, yet you'd want to taste *everything*.

"You'll have to show me your family pictures when I come over to your house," Shaundra said.

Terri tipped her glass and drank the last of the banana shake. What family pictures? They didn't even have an album. Her father carried a few school pictures of her in his wallet and that was it, except for the framed picture of her and Phil from when she was a baby. She was fat and smiling, her tongue sticking out, and her father, his cheek pressed against her cheek, had his eyes nearly closed, a big happy smile on his face.

"My father doesn't like cameras," Terri said. "It's

really funny how they bug him. We hardly ever take pictures."

"Lucky," Shaundra said. "In this family they're always snapping away. 'Smile!' Someone is always whipping out a camera. 'Smile!' Why do you have to smile when you look at a camera? I only smile when I feel like it."

"When you're feeling good," Terri agreed.

"No, sometimes I don't even smile then. Just when I feel like it. When I want to, that's when I smile." And she smiled at Terri.

A few minutes later, Shaundra's two younger brothers, Barry and Gary, came in. "Would you believe it?" Shaundra said. "Barry and Gary! My parents must have been out to lunch when they named them."

"Who's your friend, Shaundra?" Barry said, looking into her room. He was a sturdy boy of about eleven, with red, red cheeks.

"Shoo!" Shaundra said.

"I'm Terri," Terri said.

"Hi, Terri. You look nice. What are you doing with an animal like my sister?"

"Go!" Shaundra screamed.

Gary looked over his brother's shoulder. He had a thin face and big round eyes like Shaundra's.

"Let's get *out* of here," Shaundra said.

They walked over to the elementary school and sat on the monkey bars. "Wait till my mother comes home," Shaundra said, digging her hands into her hair. "She'll tell me I should have hung around and watched the Barry and Gary brats. Watched them do what? Wreck the house?"

They sat there talking. Shaundra was impressed with all the places Terri had lived. "I've never been *anywhere*."

"When your mother wants to take a trip, get her to go to Niagara Falls."

"What for, a honeymoon? Don't answer! I'm trying

35

to get over making everything into a joke. It's my worst fault. What's yours?"

"Oh . . ." Terri thought about it. "Maybe not always showing people how much I like them, when I *do* like them."

Shaudra nodded. "Did you love Niagara Falls the most of all the places you've lived?"

"It was one of the best because of the Falls. And also, Mrs. Secundo, our landlady. We lived right in her house with her. We had two rooms to ourselves, and we shared the rest of the house." She told Shaundra about Elvira Secundo, who was sixty-eight and always wore a long green cardigan that said SWEET SONIA in white lettering over the breast pocket. "She bought the sweater at the Goodwill Store."

"Oh, that's *sad,*" Shaundra said.

"I know, but it wasn't, really. She said she liked it because it was warm as a blanket. I mean, she really loved that sweater, that's why it wasn't sad."

"Maybe," Shaundra said, doubtfully. "I feel sorry for old people. It must be horrible to be old."

"I think old people are beautiful. Mrs. Secundo had so many wrinkles in her face, but she had all her own teeth. Whenever Daddy did something for her, she would take his hand and say, 'That's good, little boy, that's good.' "

"Tell me more! Listening to you is like listening to a story."

Terri was flattered and told Shaundra how any place they ever lived, she and her father would fix up things. At Mrs. Secundo's they had grouted the bathroom tiles, built shelves, and even cut a new window in her kitchen to bring in more light.

"You did it, too?" Shaundra said.

"Well, naturally, Daddy did most of the work, but I was his helper. I used to just fetch Daddy's tools, but now I can do different things. A lot of times I do the measuring for a job, and I can hammer and saw pretty good."

36

"You could be a carpenter!" Shaundra said. "That's won—oh, *look,* Terri. Check out that guy over there playing basketball. Woo woo, he's taking off his shirt. Hi, Sweetie! Come on over here. I want to talk to you."

"He heard you," Terri said, straight-faced.

"He did!" Shaundra gasped. "You creep, he did not! Do you have a boyfriend, Terri?"

"No."

"I bet you like someone, though?"

Terri nodded, trying not to laugh.

"Who is he? Tell me who he is. I'll rate him for you."

"Well . . . I don't want him to know."

"I won't tell," Shaundra said. "I may talk a lot, but I know how to keep a secret. Give me a clue."

"He plays in the band."

"What else?"

"He has a wristwatch with a stretch band and wears sneakers without socks."

"Why, now I'd know him anywhere. Just tell me a few more little details. Why don't you start with his name?"

"Uh, well, it's George—"

"George? What instrument does he play?"

"Uh, well, the oboe."

"George Torrance? Him, Terri? He's so skinny and he has greasy hair."

"No, he doesn't. Anyway, that's superficial, Shaundra. His eyes are beautiful. Don't you think his eyes are beautiful?"

"How can you tell behind those glasses? Listen, you just can't get anything going with George because what if you married—*Terri Torrance?*"

"I'll put off the wedding plans," Terri said. "What about you? Do you have a boyfriend?"

"Oh, *me.*" Shaundra grabbed her hair. "I'm boy crazy. Well, semi-boy crazy. I have six boys I like."

"*Six?*"

"I told you, I'm terrible." Shaundra dug around in

37

her pocket. "Want a chocolate mint? Oh, yuck, they're all melted."

"It still tastes good," Terri said, putting the mint into her mouth.

"Want to know something, Terri? I wanted to talk to you before yesterday."

"You did? You never said anything."

"Well, I didn't know if you really liked me. Sometimes you seemed real cool."

"I'm not cool," Terri said. "You know, not inside. I was worried about you."

"*Me?* But I'm so friendly." Shaundra lolled her tongue at the corner of her mouth and panted like a little dog. "Isn't it gross the way people are always worrying about what other people think of them?"

"I know, but it's hard to help it."

"Maybe for kids, but what about when you're grown up?" Shaundra split the last mint in half. "What's the point of even growing up, if you still go around moaning and groaning? It's bad enough being our age and feeling so insecure. You should hear my mother every time she has to sub at a new school. 'Oh! oh! what if those kids don't like me?' I always tell her, 'Relax, Ma, they're *not* going to like you. Kids *hate* substitutes.' "

"I don't think my father worries about stuff like that," Terri said. "He's usually sort of confident, but sometimes—*his* worst fault is that he might not want to talk about what I want to talk about."

"Oh, I can't stand it when people clam up," Shaundra said. "In case you haven't noticed it, talking must be my favorite thing in the world. Too bad they don't have fitness tests in talking. I'd be a ten."

They were both laughing. Shaundra put her hand on Terri's arm. "I have this feeling—do you have it? We're going to be best friends. Don't you think so?"

Terri thought of the long trail of best friends behind her: Susan Whittacker in Boston, Enid Cohen in Dallas, Jeannie Whizenand in that little town called Sterling . . . and Rachey Stevenson, and Nini, and Jennifer, and Holly. "I hope so," she said.

"Is that all?" Shaundra looked disappointed.

Terri squeezed her hand. "I like you. I like you a lot. I *do* want to be best friends."

"Then we will be," Shaundra said. "And that's all there is to it!"

Five

Lunch hour and still warm enough to eat outside. Terri leaned back on the step, waiting for Shaundra. The sun in her eyes made her feel sleepy. The night before she'd had *the dream* again. It was always the same. Her father was leaving her, she ran after him, calling his name, but he was gone, and she was alone. Sometimes in the dream she was in a house, sometimes walking down a dark street, but always alone. And it was the alone feeling she would wake up with. Dreams were supposed to mean something about your life, but this dream didn't make sense. Her father had never left her.

She saw Shaundra coming around the side of the building and waved. "Were you waiting long?" Shaundra sat down, rolling up the sleeves of her checked shirt. "Higgens was having a temper tantrum and didn't let us go when the bell rang."

Shaundra unwrapped her sandwich. "I just love the man. You know how he flings out his arms? Well, today he leaped right up on his chair. Oh, ugh, tuna fish," she said, taking a bite.

They had been friends now for nearly a month. They ate lunch together every day and went to each other's houses after school whenever they could. Shaundra had a Mickey Mouse pin, and gave it to Terri. Terri had a friendship ring, and gave it to Shaundra. Shaundra said Terri's present was much better, but Terri loved the Mickey Mouse pin, which was just the head of

Mickey with big white ears, and wore it all the time on her sweaters or pinned to her bookbag.

"My mother's idea of a heavenly lunch," Shaundra said, taking another bite of her sandwich. "Why can't she get it through her head I hate tuna fish?"

"I'll trade with you," Terri said.

"You will? You *are* a good friend."

After school they met by the bicycle rack. "Guess what Higgens gave us for our assignment?" Shaundra said as they got on their bikes. "Three hundred words on our earliest memory. Now I ask you. Could you tell *which* memory is your first?"

"Mmm," Terri said, aware that for her it wasn't which memory to choose, but to find *any* early memory. When she looked back and tried to remember things from before she was in school, it was like staring into a dark, dark room. A room you sensed wasn't empty, but where you couldn't see anything. Sometimes, just once in a great while, there was a swift, tiny flash of light into that darkness. It could be words. *Daddy's girl . . . you're Daddy's girl . . . drink this orange pop . . . Daddy's girl likes orange pop . . .* Or a feeling-memory. *Sick to her stomach . . . the rocking of a car . . . crying . . .* or words again. *Mommy, want Mommy . . . Mommy . . .*

"So, what's *your* first memory?" Shaundra said.

"Uh, oh . . ." Terri groped, thought of pale orange light sliding in through the window of a car . . . orange light on an orange can . . .

"See," Shaundra said, "you don't know, either."

"Yes, I do." Her voice sounded too loud. "My first memory is of, of an orange. Peeling an orange and eating it. I've always loved oranges," she added, wondering if that sounded convincing, like a real memory. It must have been okay, because Shaundra didn't challenge it.

Halfway up Dunn Street Hill Shaundra got off her bike and pushed. Terri took off her corduroy jacket,

41

stuffed it into the saddle bag, then stood up on the pedals. "You could walk faster," Shaundra said.

"I know." She hated to give up too easily. A car passed, and the driver looked out at her. Terri hardly saw the woman, only caught a glint of light off her sunglasses, but for an instant that dark room in her mind lit up. It must have been the strange state of mind she was still in from her dream. She saw yellow sunglasses sitting on a bureau, then sneakers. Yellow sneakers. Yellow glasses and yellow sneakers.

"Turkey," Shaundra taunted, looking back. "Why don't you get a horse?"

Fixing her eyes on the crest of the hill Terri thought that if she could make it to the top she'd know what the glasses and sneakers meant. But a moment later she had to get off and push, also.

At Shaundra's house there was a note from her mother telling her to do a laundry and clean the bathroom. "And don't forget the toilet," she wrote.

"How disgusting," Shaundra said.

"I'll help you."

"You don't have to."

"I don't mind."

"Well, I'll do the yucky job. You can clean the sink and the mirror. Let's do it fast and go to your house so I don't get stuck with my gross little brothers." She started throwing things into the washing machine. Terri raced after her, throwing in more clothes and the soap powder. She slammed down the machine top, and they ran into the bathroom and began cleaning as fast as they could.

They were still laughing when they got to Terri's house about an hour later. The phone was ringing as Terri unlocked the door. "Hurry up," Shaundra said.

"The key's stuck."

The phone rang again. Barkley was scratching the door.

"I can't stand a ringing phone," Shaundra moaned.

"It's not for you," Terri said, giving the key a hard twist. "It's probably a wrong number, anyway."

"That doesn't matter. Coming! Coming!" Shaundra yelled. "Run, Terri!"

Terri walked into the kitchen with Barkley following, licking her hand, and picked up the phone. "Hello. Mueller residence. Terri speaking."

"Terri speaking," Shaundra whispered, rolling her eyes. "Should I feed Barkley?"

Terri nodded and pointed to the refrigerator. "Terri?" she heard. "Hello, darling!"

"Aunt Vivian!" She hadn't heard her aunt's voice for a year, but she would have recognized it anywhere. Aunt Vivian was tiny, under five feet, but there was nothing tiny about her voice. "Hello!" she said, gladly. "It's my Aunt Vivian," she told Shaundra.

"Terri, darling, I'm coming to see you soon. Will I recognize you, or have you grown up entirely?"

"I'm still me, Aunt Vivian. Taller, I guess. It's so *good* to hear your voice again."

"Darling, have you got a piece of paper? I want to give you my flight number and the date—"

"Wait, Aunt Vivian—Shaundra, give me some paper," she said. "Okay, I'm ready, Aunt Vivian." She wrote down the information. "Daddy and I will be at the airport to pick you up."

"I'll be standing on tiptoes."

Terri laughed. "You still remember that?" Once, when she was small, waiting with her father in the airport, she hadn't been able to spot her aunt in the crowd. She had been on the verge of tears. "She isn't here! She didn't come!" A moment later her aunt had appeared, and Terri, half-furious, half-relieved, had cried accusingly, "You better stand on your tiptoes next time!"

"I wish I could see you right this moment," she said, now. "What are you wearing? Is it hot in California?"

"About seventy degrees. Very nice. How is it there?"

"It's beautiful. It's fall. Where are you calling from, Aunt Vivian? Work?" Her aunt clerked in a shoe store.

"No, darling, I'm calling from a phone booth."

"Why?"

"Why?" She half laughed. "What is this, twenty questions? I don't have a phone in my, ah, apartment. Terri, did I tell you I love you?"

"I love you, too, Aunt Vivian." She glanced at Shaundra, wondering why her aunt had sounded so funny about the phone booth. Uneasy. Or maybe, embarrassed. Because she didn't have the money to have her own phone?

"Terri, it seems your father is impatient for my visit."

"We both are, Aunt Vivian."

"Yes, but there's something new, isn't there? A young woman Phil wants me to meet—"

"Nancy? How did you know about her?"

"When your father called, he mentioned her."

"Daddy called you?" Terri said, in surprise. Why hadn't he told her?

"This young woman, Nancy—she's a widow, Terri? She's all alone?"

"No, Aunt Vivian, she's divorced, and she has a little boy, Leif."

"Leif? What an odd name. How do you feel about her? Do you like her?"

"Yes, I do. I like her a lot."

"That's good. That part is good." She fell silent. Terri wondered which part wasn't good. "So it's serious?" she said, in a moment. "Well, I thought so when Phil called." Her voice trailed off, then came back strong again. "Well, we'll talk about everything when I'm there. Good-by for now, darling."

"Good-by, Aunt Vivian." She didn't hang up until she heard the phone click on the other end. Then, just as she put the receiver into the cradle, she thought of something and said, "Aunt Vivian? Aunt Vivian?" The connection was broken. She hung up, thinking that her

44

aunt had said she was calling from a booth because she didn't have a phone in her apartment. But then how had Terri's father known where to phone her? It didn't make sense unless Aunt Vivian had called him first and arranged with him to call *her* back. But why would they do things in such a complicated way?

Then she thought how, once a year, there was Aunt Vivian's phone call to say, "I'm coming." And then she was here—wherever the *here* was for Terri and Phil —for a few days. And then she was gone. And then, no word until the next year, the next call, the next visit.

They weren't a letter-writing family. She couldn't remember ever seeing a letter to or from her aunt. But then how did her aunt always know where they were, even though it was always somewhere different from the year before? Did her father write her without Terri's knowledge? Had he called Vivian more than this one time without telling Terri? Did he, in fact, telephone his sister regularly without telling her? The whole train of thought was really upsetting and uncomfortable for Terri.

Then something else she had almost forgotten flashed into her mind. The year before at Christmas she had told her father she wanted to send her aunt a card. He had said, "Sure thing," but about a week later when she asked for Vivian's address, he had said, "I thought you wanted *me* to do it, Terr. I sent her a card the other day."

Standing there now, staring at the mute phone, Terri remembered exactly how casually her father had said that. And how equally casually she had said, "Oh, sure, that's okay." She'd put the card away and forgotten about it. Forgotten, too, how in some tiny, almost hidden-from-herself part of her mind, she had known that her father *had not wanted* to give her Vivian's address.

"That must have been your favorite aunt," Shaundra said.

Terri started. She'd nearly forgotten Shaundra, who

45

was sitting on the edge of the table, swinging her legs. Barkley was lying on the floor at her feet. "She's my only aunt."

"Your only? How can she be your only? I have ten aunts. You have anything to eat in this house? I'm starved. Can I have an apple?"

Terri polished two Macintosh apples on her sleeve and explained to Shaundra that Vivian was her father's only (and older) sister, and that her mother had had no sisters, or brothers either. "And I'm an only. And probably when I get married, I'll only have one child, too." Was she talking too much? Better than listening to the disturbing thoughts in her head.

"Just one aunt and no uncles? How about greats? You know, your parents' aunts and uncles?"

Terri bit into the apple. "I don't have any of those, either. You talk, Shaundra, as if you expect everyone to have an enormous family like you."

"I do?" Shaundra's eyes opened wide. "No, I don't. Where does your aunt live?"

"California. Isn't this apple good?"

"My Aunt Lucille and Uncle Dave live in Encino. Where exactly does your aunt live in California?"

"I don't know," Terri said.

"What do you mean, you don't know?"

"What do *you* mean, what do I mean, I don't know? Just don't," Terri said, but it occurred to her that not knowing where her aunt lived was either very dumb, or something else awfully strange. "I suppose, Shaundra, you know where all your many aunts and uncles live?"

"Well, not all of them. But I have a few more to keep track of than you do, Terri Mueller."

Terri threw her apple core into the garbage. "What should we do? We're just hanging around." She scrubbed potatoes and put them in the stovetop baker. "Barkley, get out from under my feet!"

"Why are you yelling at Barkley? Are you getting mad?" Shaundra said. "You sound mad."

"Who's mad?" Terri went into her room and stretched out on her bed, her legs dangling over the edge. Why did she feel so disagreeable?

"Where's your Aunt Vivian going to sleep?" Shaundra said, standing in the doorway. "On the couch?"

"Are you kidding? That mangy old thing? Right here. We have a folding cot. I'll take the cot and give her my bed."

"Good luck. You'll be stepping on each other's faces." She picked up a bunch of keys from the bureau. "What're all these?"

"You saw them before," Terri said. "They're from all the different houses and places we've lived."

"You never told me that."

"I did, too."

"You didn't. But it's neat, anyway. You're lucky, I've never been anywhere."

"You *always* say that! It's not such a big deal. Anyway, you exaggerate *everything*. I know you've been plenty of places!"

There was a moment's silence, then Shaundra said, "You're being such a grouch. Ever since your aunt called. I thought you were happy she's coming."

"I am!" Terri picked furiously at the binding on her blanket. What could she say? How could she tell Shaundra that questions were blowing through her mind like a wind storm. Why didn't *they* ever visit Aunt Vivian? Had her father really sent that Christmas card? Why didn't he like to talk about her mother? Where were her little-girl memories? And why didn't they have even one picture of her mother?

She smelled something burning. The potatoes. She ran into the kitchen, turned down the fire. *Careful, Terri. Careful what you do. Careful what you think. Careful what you say to other people.*

"Are we having a fight?" Shaundra said, folding her arms across her chest.

Terri's heart thumped hard. "What? Why?"

47

"I don't *know* why," Shaundra said. "That's for you to say."

"I'm going to make some popcorn," Terri said, going to the cupboard. The bag slipped out of her hand. Yellow kernels slid all over the floor. Terry felt ready to cry. Barkley got excited and began nosing the kernels around.

"Klutz," Shaundra said to Terri.

"What's *that?*" They both got down on their hands and knees, chasing popcorn kernels.

"You know—a clumsy oaf," Shaundra said.

"Oh, thank you!"

Terri made popcorn and they carried the bowl into the living room and ate without talking for a few minutes. "It's good popcorn," Shaundra said, "even if it doesn't have garlic."

"I could get you some."

"No, that's all right. You don't like it."

"I don't mind." She went into the kitchen and brought back the garlic-salt shaker.

"I didn't really mean that about you being a klutz," Shaundra said.

"Well, I am, sometimes."

"No, it was mean of me to say it. You're not clumsy at all. You're very graceful."

"Well, I was acting mean to you, so I don't blame you for saying it."

They sort of smiled at each other. "I guess we're making up?" Terri said.

"I want to."

Later, looking out the window, Terri saw her father locking up the truck. She pointed him out to Shaundra.

"He's the one in the denim jacket? Coming across the street?"

"Right."

"Gee, he's cute."

"Shut up, boy crazy, that's my father."

When Phil came in, Terri introduced Shaundra.

"Hello, Mr. Mueller," she said, tucking her hair behind her ears.

"Hello, Shaundra. I've heard a lot about you."

"Same here! I mean, I've heard a lot about you. Terri talks about you all the time."

Her father laughed. "I hope she doesn't complain too much."

"Oh, no, she thinks you're wonderful. Super Dad."

Terri gave Shaundra a shove. She couldn't believe the way Shaundra was flirting.

"Do you need a ride home, Shaundra?"

"No, thanks, Mr. Mueller, I've got my bike," she said. "See you tomorrow, Terri."

Terri went to the downstairs door with Shaundra. "Your father's so nice," Shaundra whispered.

"I know, I know."

When she went back upstairs, Terri's father asked if she'd taken Barkley out yet. "I didn't get a chance, Daddy." She told him about her aunt's phone call. "She called from a phone booth."

Her father nodded. No reaction. Nothing about having called Vivian. "So she's coming? Great! Good!" And that was it. "I'm going to clean up now. Why don't you take out Barkley?"

By the time she returned from walking the dog, her father was out of the shower and changed into fresh clothes. "What should we have for supper?" he asked. "I could eat a horse."

"I started potatoes, but they're a little burned." She opened the refrigerator, but she wasn't thinking about food. All the time she'd been walking Barkley, questions about the two of them, and Aunt Vivian, and the way they lived had been going around in her mind.

"Nothing looks interesting?" her father said. "Tell you what—let's go out. I don't feel much like cooking."

Later, in the restaurant he poured a little wine into her water glass and she sipped it between bites of the veal parmigiana, which was her favorite Italian food. They talked about some place nice to take her aunt on her visit and planned to have a big family dinner with Nancy and Leif.

Driving home, Terri glanced at her father's profile, dark in the truck, and thought again of the troublesome questions. Supposing she were to ask him point blank: Why didn't you tell me you phoned Aunt Vivian? Would it sound as if she didn't trust him? She yawned. The wine had made her sleepy. Why ask anything? she thought, yawning again. Why not just let things go along as they were?

Barkley was at the door waiting for them. "What smells burned?" her father said as they walked in.

"Oops!" Terri ran into the kitchen. She'd forgotten to take the potatoes off the stove. "That makes two times today I did this!"

"Don't worry about it," her father said, dumping the burned potatoes into the garbage. "It could happen to anyone."

Terri took a deep breath. She didn't feel sleepy anymore. "Daddy," she heard herself saying. "I want to see my birth certificate."

"Your birth— Where'd that come from?"

She hesitated. Should she stop before she made a fool of herself? Or before they arrived at that point of stubborn silence where she would have to challenge him to get what she wanted? The worst part was, she didn't know exactly *what* it was that she wanted. "I want to see it," she said softly. "My birth certificate— I just want to. Okay?"

"Well, it's in the box." He kept a small, locked, grey metal box in his room with all their important papers. His Army discharge, their health insurance, tax forms, things like that. She was aware of the box, but had never seen the contents. She felt that he was waiting for her to withdraw the request.

"Can I see it?" she said again.

He shrugged. "If you want to."

"Yes. Yes, I do."

He brought the box into the kitchen, put it on the

table, and took the key from his keychain. She watched as he sorted through several manila envelopes. Then he handed her a piece of stiff paper bordered in red. She held the paper in both hands and read the words. She felt very nervous and at first it didn't make any sense.

This is to certify that Terri Lee Mueller was born . . . in the City of Oakland, California, . . . in the County of . . . to Kathryn Susso Mueller and Philip James Mueller . . . on the ninth day of April, 197— . . .

Slowly the words arranged themselves into sentences. Yes, there it was, black on white. She had been born—to a mother and a father. The only thing that actually came to as a surprise was her mother's middle name. Susso. She hadn't known that. "Was that my mother's maiden name?"

"Yes." He held out his hand for the paper and locked it back into the box. "Feel better now?" A little smile, as if they'd had a fight—no, a struggle of some sort—and he had won. She felt a kind of vague shame. *What have you found out? What difference did that make?*

But later, in bed, her eyes open, staring at the dark ceiling, the thought came to her with force that something was wrong. She had never let herself think this, in these exact words, but she felt she had known it for a long time. She thought of all her questions. She thought of their moves, how they had no place of their own, belonged nowhere special, and to no one but each other. She lay very still and thought it again. Something is wrong.

Six

"Hello?"

"Hello—is Shaundra there, is she awake?"

"Who's this?"

"Terri."

"Hi, Terri!"

"Hi, who's this?"

"Barry."

"Oh, hi, Barry, what are you doing up so early?"

"Talking to you. You called to talk to me, didn't you?"

"Well, actually, hate to disappoint you, but—"

"Hey, Terri? Guess what? I got chosen captain of the traffic patrol."

"You did! Who chose you?"

"All the other traffic patrol kids."

"That's really good, Barry. Do I have to call you Captain Barry from now on? Captain Barry, can I talk to your sister?"

"What do you want to talk to her for?"

"Captain Barry! This is General Mueller. Please get Private Shaundra at once!"

"Yes, sir, General. Bye, Terri."

"Bye, Barry."

"Hello?"

"Shaundra, it's me. Are you awake?"

"No, I'm sleeping, bozo. What time is it?"

"Six-thirty."

"Six-thirty! What are you doing up so early? I thought you didn't have to go to the airport until nine o'clock."

"I woke up and I couldn't go back to sleep. Thinking about Aunt Vivian coming—well, I just wanted to say hello to you, Shaundra, because I probably won't get to see you until Monday."

"I hope you have a wonderful time," Shaundra said. "I hope your Aunt Vivian has a wonderful time."

"We will. She will. We always do."

"How come she's only staying for the weekend, though?"

"I told you, airhead, she has a job and she can't get time off."

They talked for a few more minutes, then Terri hung up. Her father was still asleep, so she got dressed and took Barkley out for a walk. It was a still, moist autumn morning. She cut down a side street and up the hill behind the old church to the field. The sun came out and a few little clouds passed overhead. There were birds in the thorn apple trees. While Barkley ran around, very excited about being outside so early, Terri picked an armful of asters and goldenrod.

At home she put the flowers in a glass jar and set it on the bureau. They glowed and made the room look special and welcoming.

As soon as they finished breakfast she and her father put Barkley out on the enclosed back porch and drove to the airport. In the airport, Terri looked around, but didn't see her aunt. She tensed: that old unreasonable fear. Then she heard her aunt's voice, full and carrying. "Terri! Philly!" But she still didn't see her.

"Where *is* she?"

Taking Terri by the shoulders, her father turned her. There, coming through the security gate, was her aunt, completely dressed in purple and almost dwarfed by her suitcase, umbrella, and several shopping bags.

Terri ran to her, her aunt dropped everything, and

they hugged hard. "Darling! Terri!" Her aunt's eyes were wet.

"Now your turn, Philly," she said to her brother.

"Viv—" He bent down and kissed her. "So good to see you."

"And you, honey!" She took him by the shoulders and looked into his face for a long time, then, apparently satisfied, kissed him soundly on each cheek.

That done, Vivian distributed her packages—suitcase to Phil, shopping bags to Terri—and marched ahead of them out of the building toward the parking lot. Terri's father shared an amused look with her. "Vivian," he called. "You don't know where the truck is parked. Better wait for us."

"Hurry up, Philly! I don't want to waste a moment of this visit."

Her aunt was under five feet, but Terri had long ago noticed that she never acted short or small. She had a big voice and lots of strong opinions which she didn't hesitate to air. And besides this, she never let Terri's father forget that he was her younger brother. She insisted on calling him Philly.

"Viv," Phil Mueller said as they drove home, "you make me feel like a baseball team. How about doing me the favor of calling me Phil or Philip."

"You know how many years you've been saying that same thing?" She squeezed Terri's arm to her side. "I don't see any reason to stop calling you Philly. It's just my affectionate name for my kid brother."

"How do you expect my daughter to respect me when she hears me called a kid brother?"

"Well, that's what you are, Philly, and that's what you're going to remain, no matter how old you get!"

"You two," Terri said, happily. Her father's and her aunt's bickering made her feel as if hardly any time had passed since Vivian's last visit. She inched closer to her aunt. It was so good having her here. She wanted to savor every moment. She had been thinking about asking her aunt some of the questions that were bothering her, but she was afraid that would change things. Aunt Vivian's visit was for enjoyment and happiness.

At home, while Aunt Vivian unpacked in her room, Terri and her father made lunch. "Pastrami sandwich, Viv?" Phil called.

"Not with my ulcer, Phil," she said, coming into the kitchen. She set a bottle of Maalox on the counter and put the teakettle on to boil. "Tea and cottage cheese will do for me." She'd brought a little packet of an herbal tea called Red Zinger.

"It's really red," Terri said.

"Try it, darling, it's lovely."

They talked about Terri's school. Her aunt wanted to know about every class and how Terri was doing, and then all about Shaundra. "So she has two little brothers?"

"Well, not that little. Barry is eleven."

"Well, poor Barry," Phil said. "He'll get to be thirty-five and as far as his older sister is concerned he'll still be in short pants."

Vivian laughed. "That's right. You little brothers can never catch up with your big sisters."

"Not in years, maybe," Terri's father said.

"Not in anything. I'll always have more experience and more wisdom than you."

Phil Mueller's laugh exploded. "Vivian, you're not only stubborn, you're downright unbearable."

She stirred her tea. "No, I'm serious. Every year you live, you learn more things. I'm ten years older than you, you can't get away from that. That gives me a perspective you don't have."

Terri, slathering mustard on her sandwich, was aware of the crackle of some real tension between her father and her aunt. *Secrets. They've got secrets*. The thought came unbidden. It fell into place next to *something is wrong*.

Nothing on her aunt's visit went the way Terri had thought it would. Perhaps it was her? Terri herself? She kept seeing and hearing things in ways she wouldn't have only a year ago. Did a year make that much difference? And then, too, all the plans they'd made with Nancy had to be scrapped, because a few days before, Nancy had come down with a hard case of the flu.

Later that afternoon they drove over to Nancy's so Vivian could at least meet her. Nancy was lying on the couch in a plaid bathrobe. "You don't feel any better?" Phil said, kissing her.

"At least . . . I'm back with the living," Nancy croaked. "You should have seen me yesterday." She held out a limp hand to Vivian. "I'm really glad to meet you."

"Well! So you're Nancy." Vivian looked all around. The apartment was a mess. Leif was sitting on the couch next to his mother with his thumb stuck in his mouth. The shades were drawn. Terri was reminded that the week before when she'd come over to babysit, Nancy had said, "Frankly, Terri, I'm real anxious about meeting your aunt. She's so important to Phil. I'm going to go all out to make a positive impression."

"Poor Nancy," Terri said. Her hair looked sticky, her nose was red, and her big wonderful eyes were half-swollen.

"I know, I look *terrible,*" she said. She blew her nose. There was a wastebasket full of used tissues next to her.

Terri indicated Leif's thumb. "I didn't know he did that."

"Oh . . . just when he gets upset." Nancy's voice trailed away. She looked pretty upset herself.

They stood around for a few minutes, making talk about the weather and Aunt Vivian's plane trip. Then Nancy said in an exhausted voice, "You guys go. I'm not fit company." Phil kissed her again, and they all trailed out.

"She seems very nice," Vivian said when they were in the truck, but the way she said it, Terri wasn't sure if she meant it.

"Nancy's usually *much* nicer," she said. "She's never

56

quiet like today. She must really be sick. I never saw Nancy so blah."

"Terri's right," her father said. "It was an awful way for you to meet her, Viv."

"I'm sure . . ." She started asking questions about Nancy—how old she was, where her family lived, and how she supported herself and Leif. She didn't say anything outright negative, but Phil sounded edgy as he answered, and Terri felt right in the middle. By the time they got home everyone was in a grouchy mood. Her father turned on the TV and her aunt stretched out on the couch saying she must be having jet lag.

"Terri, would you get my cigarettes? I have a pack of Players in my purse. It's on your bureau, dear."

"You should stop smoking, Viv," her father said.

"Well, I've tried, dear, but when I get nervous I want a cigarette."

"I'm sure it's not good for your ulcer, either."

"Now, Philly—"

"I'll get the cigarettes," Terri said hastily. In her room she poked around in Aunt Vivian's pocketbook— it was more like a huge carpetbag with wooden handles, full of a jumble of things. As she fumbled inside, Vivian's wallet fell open and Terri saw a picture of her aunt, standing in front of a house with two cute grinning boys, neither much older than she was, both with their arms around Vivian.

Terri stared. Who were they? Were they brothers? They looked alike and stood slouched on one hip in exactly the same easy manner. Did they work in the shoe store with her aunt? There was something careless about the way they stood with her between them, as if they'd known her for a long time.

The plastic envelope fell over and there was another picture, this one of a man in a green shirt, holding up a fish. Stop, she told herself, you are snooping, but she kept staring at first one picture, then the other. Who were these people? Why did Vivian have their pictures in her wallet? She flipped the plastic envelopes rapidly.

More pictures . . . no one she knew . . . naturally. But why did Aunt Vivian have these pictures in her wallet and not a single one of her or her father? Weren't *they* all Aunt Vivian had in the world, just as *she* was all they had?

"Terri?" Aunt Vivian called. "Did you find them?"

"Yes. Coming." Disturbed, she took out the cigarettes and closed the wooden handles.

Sunday morning when she woke up she saw that her aunt was also awake. She sat up, pushing the hair out of her face. "Good morning, Aunt Vivian."

"Good morning, darling. Did you sleep well on that cot?"

"Oh, fine," Terri said.

Aunt Vivian lit a cigarette. "It's sweet of you to let me have your bed."

"No, I'm glad to do it. It's nice waking up with someone else right here to talk to." She yawned and pushed her pillow up behind her head. Then, coming more awake, she said, "Aunt Vivian? Could I ask you something?"

"Of course." She pursed her lips and blew a smoke ring.

For a moment Terri was distracted. "I didn't know you could do that!" Vivian grinned and blew another ring, but this one was only half-formed.

"We all have our little talents," she said. "What'd you want to ask, dear?"

"Did you know my mother?"

"Mmm." Vivian bent over to tap ashes into an ashtray on the floor.

"What did she look like?"

"Well—" Vivian straightened up. "A tall, handsome woman. That's what I'd say."

"Do I look like her?"

"Oh, Terri . . . I don't know. It was so long ago . . ." Her voice became uncharacteristically vague. She put out her cigarette and, getting out of bed, pulled on a purple kimono. "I better get my shower now before

58

Phil gets up and there's a rush on the bathroom." She dug around in her carpetbag. "I hope I didn't forget my shower cap. Oh, here——"

"Aunt Vivian." Terri swung her legs over the side of the cot. "I want to ask you some other things."

"Mmm, what's that, dear?" Her back turned, Vivian rummaged in her suitcase.

"I've been wondering about a lot of things. What happened to the man who ran his car into my mother's car?"

Vivian looked over her shoulder at Terri. "What are you asking? Why do you bring this up?"

"There are so many things I don't know," Terri said. "I don't even know how old my mother was when——"

Turning away, her hands tucked into the sleeves of the kimono, Vivian said, "Terri, you should ask Phil whatever you want to know. It's not up to me to say." She took her clothes and left.

Terri thought of that day she had tried riding her bike to the top of Dunn Street Hill, her heart beating hard, her legs tiring, but thinking that sheer stubbornness would somehow get her to the top. Well, it hadn't. And maybe trying to find out about the past was the same thing. She just wasn't going to be successful, no matter how hard she tried.

Sunday dinner was their last meal together. Her aunt was going on an early plane the next morning. It seemed to Terri that Vivian had hardly arrived, and now she was leaving again, leaving for another year.

"I wish you didn't have to go," she said. The meal was special—steak, sweet potatoes, and hot biscuits—but she didn't feel hungry.

"Viv will be back to visit again," her father said.

"Yes. Next year."

"I wish I could visit you more often, Terri darling."

"Why can't you?" Her throat was full. Nobody answered.

Later, she found it hard to fall asleep. She lay in bed for a long time, hearing her father and Aunt Vivian talking in the living room. She was drifting off when she heard the clatter of cups in the kitchen and came awake again. Her aunt's visit had been different from other years. Not as good, not as wonderful. It wasn't her aunt's fault. It's me, Terri thought again. I'm different. It made her sad, and she got out of bed wanting to see her aunt again, to tell her that she loved her. *That* hadn't changed.

She opened her bedroom door and heard her aunt saying, "Philly, listen to me, dear, it can't go on like this. You have got to tell her."

"No," her father said.

"She's asking questions. And now you're talking about involving two more lives—"

"Viv, I can't. Think what you're saying."

"Think what you're doing, Philly."

"I have. I thought about it a long time ago."

"That's just the point—it was a long time ago. Terri's growing up. You—"

"All the more reason I can't. It's *done*."

"She has to know sometime."

Terri stood frozen by the door.

"You don't know what you're saying, Vivian."

"Things have changed, time has passed. I feel very strongly about this. I love Terri—"

"Yes, and so do I. For god's sake, do you doubt that?"

"Then tell her the truth."

"No," he said again. "Vivian—I can't."

"Then maybe I should."

There was silence. The hairs all over Terri's arms stood up.

"You've never betrayed me. You can't now." Her father's voice was low. Was he crying? She couldn't bear to hear any more and closed the door.

60

Seven

"Hand me that wrench, will you, Terri?" Phil Mueller was lying on his back on the floor, his head inside the sink cabinet.

"Do you have enough light?" Kneeling, she poked the lead light farther under the sink.

"Fine." Her father grunted as he twisted the wrench around the trap.

"Should we let the landlord know we have a leak?"

"Are you kidding? We'd be lucky if it got fixed by next spring." He crawled out from under the sink. "That should do it, but put the pan under again, just in case—"

"Daddy." She meant to speak sharply to get his attention, but the words came soft and slow. "I heard you and Aunt Vivian talking." He was washing his hands with the R&O Soap from the blue tin. "I heard you," she said. "Sunday night—before Aunt Vivian left. I heard you talking . . . I heard what you said."

"You heard us?" There was a shy smile on his face. Was it a smile? It caught her by surprise and it hurt her as if the smile were saying, *Please protect me.*

"Daddy . . ." Oh, this was so hard to do. Should she be saying these things? But if she didn't, then it would all just keep going endlessly around in her head. "I know something is wrong," she said. That sounded so bold. "I think something is wrong," she said, softly.

"Please, if it is, tell me? If you did something . . . I don't care what you did—"

"Nothing is wrong, nothing is wrong," he said. He put damp hands on her shoulders. "Do you love me?"

Why did he ask that? He knew. But he waited for her answer. She nodded. *"Yes."*

"Then that's all that matters. It's worth everything."

What was worth everything? What was the "everything"? She had spoken so softly. Maybe he hadn't really understood what she said. "I *heard* you," she said again. "You and Aunt Vivian. She said you should tell me—"

He cut her off. "That conversation wasn't meant for your ears. It was private, between me and Vivian. Were you eavesdropping? I'm disappointed in you!"

She could hardly breathe. "I wasn't eavesdropping!" Behind him, on the counter, the TV was on. Little figures danced on the screen, throwing out their arms, all of them smiling. In the background someone was singing, "Ain't life wunnerful? Wunnerful? Wunner . . . fulllll!"

"You're only thirteen," he said. "There are a lot of things in life you don't have to think about yet. Enjoy your life now, Terri, there's a long time ahead of you when things won't be nearly as much fun for you as they are now."

"I can't have fun if you're in trouble."

"I'm not in trouble," he said. His voice softened. "You can rest easy on that, honey. Look, you overheard something and you're jumping to conclusions. I think we should end this discussion." He turned away to dry his hands. "Just forget what you heard, Terri. Just forget it, honey. That's the best thing to do."

That was Wednesday night. She didn't "just forget it." She couldn't. He'd always said they shared everything. She had believed it. Didn't everything that affected him affect her? They were a *family*. But he had secrets from her. Was he protecting her from something bad or ugly?

62

She remembered a long-ago hot spring day (she'd been eight or nine), a traffic jam, cars stopped on a highway. They had walked forward. She saw the flashing lights. She saw the police cars. She saw the grey car crumpled like a piece of paper. She saw feet sticking out from beneath that crumpled paper car.

"Look, Daddy—"

"Don't!" He pulled her against him, covered her eyes, turned her, walked her away. Then, only then, she understood that she had seen death. Dead Feet. She stumbled along next to him, her face buried in his waist, her heart beating so softly and heavily inside her chest. A Dead Person. Dead like her mother. "Don't think about it," her father said. "You don't have to think about it."

But she had thought about it. Yes, even then, when she was a child. Now she was thirteen, and he was still saying the same thing to her. No good, she thought.

Friday night he went out to visit Nancy. Terri stayed home. About half an hour after he left she went to her father's room and took the grey metal box down from the closet shelf. She pressed the latch. It was locked. She pressed it again, harder.

She heard something in the hall and stopped, her heart jumping. What if her father walked in on her? Okay, she just wanted to see her birth certificate again. She'd ask him to let her have it. She would take good care of it. It was the only thing she knew of that linked her to her mother.

"Kathryn Susso Mueller," she said out loud. "Kathryn Susso. Kathy." Or maybe she had been called Kate? Or Cat? She pushed at the lock again, then put the box back. She felt restless and strange.

In the kitchen she bit into an apple. Maybe she was hungry? But after two bites she was full.

In the living room she fell down on the couch. A cloud of dust and dog hairs rose and settled. Barkley grinned hopefully at her. He wanted to play. Terri closed her eyes and tried to see her mother. *A tall, handsome woman* . . . It wasn't enough. So many things she didn't know, would never know unless someone told her. But who? Her father wouldn't talk about Kathryn.

Kathryn. She loved the name. She said it again. "Kathryn." Kathryn had been killed in her car by another driver. Had he been drunk? She *hated* that man, whoever he was. Where was he now? What if she met him someday and knew he was the one who had killed her mother?

She sat up, clutching a pillow. She would want to kill *him!* Barkley poked his head against her hand and whined. "No, Barkley, honey, not you." She put her arms around his neck. What if her father had felt this way after her mother's death? What if he had found the driver and killed him?

She jumped to her feet, turned on the TV, immediately turned it off. She had never seen Phil angry enough to even raise his voice. What had he said to her the other day? *I'm disappointed in you.* That was the way Phil got mad. But yet, the thought made so much sense, would explain so many things, that she kept thinking about it.

Say her father just hit the man. And the man slipped, fell, and cracked his head on the pavement. Died. Became a Dead Person. That would be murder. Manslaughter. What had Aunt Vivian said? *You have to tell her. She's got to know sometime* . . .

"Oh, Barkley." She put her face against his familiar stinky dog smell. "Oh, Barkley." Her father, a murderer. It would have meant jail for him. And there she would have been, four years old, with no mother and no father.

Rather than let her be orphaned, had her father decided to run? To go away with her? To disappear before the police came for him? Wasn't that it? It would explain everything. All the moves they'd made, and what her aunt had said to him, and why he didn't want

64

her to know about any of it. "Oh, Barkley," she said again.

On Saturday, Terri and Shaundra shopped in the Mall for a birthday present for Shaundra's mother. They looked at scarves, sprayed perfume on their wrists, and checked out the beads and rings in The Carousel. Finally Shaundra settled on wooden wind chimes which she said her mother could hang outside her bedroom window.

They went into Wendy's for lunch, taking a booth near the back. "What a relief to have that over with," Shaundra said. She poured ketchup on her burger. "You're sort of super-quiet today, Terri. You okay?"

"Yes, sure. I have things on my mind."

"All the cares of the world. Tell Aunt Shaundra your troubles, my child." She grabbed Terri's arm. "Terri, there goes George Torrance!"

"Where?" Terri's face warmed.

"Over there, walking past the pretzel shop. Oh my god, he's stopping to buy a pretzel."

"Don't point, Shaundra."

"I'm not *pointing*. Do you think he sees us? Do you see him? Do you *see* him?"

"I see him," Terri said. "He's with Christopher."

"Isn't he *darling?*" Shaundra said.

"George or Christopher?"

"Both of them!"

"I thought you said George had greasy hair."

"I've changed my mind. I think he's very nice. I was talking to him the other day, and I decided I'm going to do everything I can to bring you two together."

"Shaundra! You didn't say anything about me?"

"Don't worry, I'm not that dumb."

Terri slid her bracelets up and down her arm. "Shaundra—we are best friends, aren't we?"

"Yes, of course." Shaundra bit into her hamburger. "That's why I like George now."

"Yes, but I don't mean that. We should be able to tell each other anything, don't you think?"

"Yes," Shaundra said with her mouth full. "Aren't you going to eat?"

Terri took a small bite of her cheeseburger. "I want to ask you something. What if someone you thought you knew everything about . . . really knew . . . what if you found out that person did something that was, that was *bad?*"

Shaundra leaned forward. "Terri, are you in trouble?"

"No, not *me.* Someone else. What if it was your father that did the something bad—"

"He did," Shaundra said. "He divorced my mother!"

"I mean something much worse."

"What's worse than that? Murder?"

Terri set her bun down on the plate. The smell of the fried potatoes rising from the paper cone made her feel nauseous. She pushed them away.

"Hey, Terri—" Shaundra slid down in her seat. "Are you sick or something? You don't look too good."

"Shaundra—if I tell you something, will you swear never to tell anyone?" Shaundra nodded. "You've got to swear," Terri said. Shaundra nodded again and held up her hand. Terri didn't want to think about her father by herself anymore. She told Shaundra what she had overheard and what she had figured out. It was hard to say. "I think . . . my father killed that man." She wanted to call the words back.

"Terri, do you really think it happened that way?" There were little dots of sweat on Shaundra's upper lip.

"I don't know—" She felt like crying. "I don't know, but what else could it be?"

"Oh, god," Shaundra said. "That's terrible." She leaned forward. "I've heard my father say there's murder in everyone's heart. I thought that was gross, but maybe it's true. Oh, Terri. I don't know what to say."

Terri turned her head. "Don't say anything. I don't want to talk about it anymore."

"All right, we won't then. We'll talk about other stuff. I'll tell you about my seven loves."

"Seven?" Terri managed a weak smile. "I thought it was six."

"There's a new one. Rory Ross. Isn't that sweet?"

Terri smiled, a forced smile. She hardly heard anything Shaundra said. Had she made a bad mistake telling Shaundra her father's secret? If the police found out, they would come for him. She pushed aside the cold cheeseburger. The congealed meat spilling out of the bun looked like blood. Where was her father now? Home? With Nancy? Doing their shopping? It didn't matter. If the police wanted him, they'd find him. She had told Shaundra too much. Shaundra's father was a policeman.

What if Shaundra said to him, *Pop, I have a friend who thinks her father killed someone a long time ago.* And what if Shaundra's father, the detective father, said, *This sounds like an interesting case . . .* and came with a gun and handcuffs . . .

"Daddy." Her lips silently formed the word. *Daddy, you're right, I don't have to know . . . whatever you did, keep the secret. Don't tell me. I don't care. Let's just go, let's leave this town, let's go right now so they won't ever find you . . .*

"Terri. Terri?" Shaundra shook her arm. "What's the *matter?*"

"I was just . . ." Her palms were soaked. "I was just thinking . . . Shaundra, you won't ever say anything about my father to anyone?"

"I told you I wouldn't, Terri."

"Not anyone?"

"I won't. I *promise* you. I won't! Please don't feel so bad. Maybe it's not what you said at all. You know, you said yourself your father couldn't hurt anyone." She put her hand over Terri's and Terri felt comforted for the moment, and close to her friend.

Eight

"Okay, class," Mr. Higgens said, "settle down." Tall, gaunt, with strings of wispy hair plastered to his skull, he was Terri's favorite teacher. "I hope you have all come prepared to write an article for our newspaper. Remember, the paper we're going to put together in the next couple weeks will include everything covered by a regular newspaper. Features, sports stories, cartoons, plenty of columns. Who's going to be our Ann Landers? Volunteers? No? Lizbet?" He grinned fiercely at a big blonde girl sitting near the window. "We'll call it Dear Lizbet."

"Not me," Lizbet said, reddening.

"We're going to put out a newspaper," Mr. Higgens went on, unperturbed, "and it's going to be *interesting*. Nothing boring for us. Our articles are going to be written with verve, style, and wit. Everybody ready to be witty and stylish? Not to speak of vervish?"

Terri laughed along with everyone else, enjoying Mr. Higgens' performance. He rubbed his hands together. "Now, to sell this paper, what we really need is a nice juicy murder story on page one to grab our readers."

Terri's enjoyment vanished abruptly. For a few moments she had managed to forget about her father. Now it all came back. A feeling of frustration and nothingness swept over her. She sat up rigidly. She had to *think*, not drown in a sea of self-pity. This morning, Shaundra had said, "Grown-ups want you to turn off

68

your mind. Thirteen? So what? They think thirteen is still sucking your thumb."

At home, Terri's father acted as he always did . . . but, perhaps, not exactly. She'd caught him looking at her a bit more keenly than usual, almost measuring her. Was he wondering if she had followed orders? *Forget it, Terri,* he'd said.

She doodled on notepaper, wrote "Daddy," and next to it, "Terri," then cartooned a little tyke clutching at her father's knee with an amiable grin. "I am your typical good little girl," she wrote in a balloon over the little tyke's head. Then, a few strokes of the pencil and the little tyke's grin turned a shade evil. The little tyke was up to no good—Daddy better watch out!

"All right," Mr. Higgens was saying, "we can democratically elect an editor"—applause from the class—"or I can in typical, tyrannical fashion appoint myself. I appoint myself. Call me Ace. And remember, all you Woodwards and Bernsteins, we need feature stories. Terri, are you with us today?"

She looked up, nodded. "I'm here."

"I have a feeling you were mulling over an idea for a feature story?"

She shook her head. But a headline leaped into her mind. *How My Father Avenged My Mother's Death.*

"Well, put your quiet little mind to it, please." He turned his gaze on another victim. "You there, Robert Olesky, what does your fertile brain think would make a good feature story? Remember, features should have heart, soul, and body."

"And bloo-ood," Kenny Collins said from the back of the room.

Everyone was laughing. Terri's thoughts ran in a jumbled rush, from news stories, to blood, to the metal box, to the manila envelopes. What was in the box? An Army discharge. An insurance policy. What else? What if there were newspaper clippings? *Oakland Woman Dies in Car Crash. Death Car Driver Dies in Mysterious Accident. Husband of Dead Woman Sought.*

She bent over her paper. She was so slow! Why had it taken her all this time to realize answers to her questions were in the locked box? If only she had a key.

At the end of the day Shaundra met her at her locker.

"Hi. What's happening?" They walked out through the big front doors. "Let's do something. What should we do?"

"I don't know, what do you want to do?" Terri said. Could she have a key made? In stories people were always making wax impressions of keys.

"Let's go to the drugstore and look at magazines."

"Okay." Or else they had sensitive fingers that knew how to make locks open with a touch.

In the drugstore they bought a bag of jelly beans and looked at *Seventeen* and *Teen Miss*.

"What now?" Shaundra said as they walked out together, eating jelly beans. A plan formed in Terri's mind. "I better go home," she said.

"I'll come with you."

"Shaundra—maybe you don't want to. I'm going to do something—" She stopped. Imagining breaking into her father's locked box was one thing. Saying it out loud, though, would be almost like doing it. And doing it? Her stomach jumped, and she wished she hadn't eaten so many jelly beans.

"What're you going to do? I'll help you. I hope it's not cleaning the bathroom."

She said it quickly. "I'm going to break into my father's locked box."

"Why?"

"I think maybe he has newspaper stories in there about my mother, and about—about the other thing—"

"The *driver?*" Shaundra said. "But, Terri, if he really did that, why would he want to keep articles about it?"

Terri walked faster. "I don't know, Shaundra. I only know I've just got to try and find out if it's true. I don't want to do this, but I can't go on not knowing."

Leaves were falling from the trees, a yellow rain of leaves. Terri felt impatient, stretched her legs. In a moment she was ahead of Shaundra. Go home, open the box, look through the envelopes. Find out, get it over with. And then she would say to her father, *You see, I know, and it's better, because now, whatever happens, it's the two of us.*

"Terri. Terri, wait!"

"Sorry." Terri slowed down. "Sorry, Shaundra. Maybe you ought to go home, because when my father finds out, you could be in trouble with your mother."

"When your father finds out?" Shaundra said. "How do you know he's going to find out?"

"He'll find out. Because I'll tell him."

Shaundra's eyes got big. "You're going to break into the box, and then *tell* him? What kind of *sense* is that?"

"Shaundra—what's the point of me doing this, trying to find out the truth, if I'm going to keep secrets, too?"

"Oh. Yeah. Well, I didn't think of *that.*"

The apartment was still, had that closed-off feeling. Terri opened a window in the kitchen, then tried another in the living room. It was stuck tight. She tugged, trying to push it up.

"What are you doing, you crazy girl? I thought you were going to open the box, not the dumb window."

Terri tugged. "I want some air. Fresh air. Don't you think this apartment smells mouldy?"

"What time does your father come home? If we're going to do the box, let's do it!"

"Once more—" This time Terri got the window open. "Are you hungry? Do you want something to eat?"

"No. Where is the stupid box?"

In Mr. Higgens' class, thinking of this moment, she had felt herself balanced as if on a sliver of glass, but now, as she took the grey box down from the closet and set it on the floor, she seemed to feel nothing, to be utterly nerveless.

They knelt down on either side of the box. It was an ordinary gun metal grey box with a small metal handle. Beneath the lock were the words Safety Lock Company in silver letters.

"Is that it?" Shaundra whispered.

"Yes." Terri's voice sounded loud. "That's it."

Suddenly Shaundra took one of the pillows off Terri's father's bed and threw it at her. Terri caught it and slung it at Shaundra. "Touch you last!"

Shaundra yelped and picked up the other pillow. They slammed each other, laughing hysterically, and finally falling on the floor.

"Maybe your father's coming home early," Shaundra said.

"He usually tells me." Terri got up and looked out the window. "He's not here yet." Then they both looked at the box again.

"Well . . . so . . . are you going to do it?" Shaundra said.

"Okay. I'm going to do it." Terri went to her room and got her jackknife. In her father's room again she went to work on the lock. Shaundra kept making bad jokes. "Real criminal stuff, Terri. I wonder how many years they'll give us."

"Shaundra, shut up," Terri said, at last. Her tongue between her teeth, she bent the lock. A little more pressure, and it snapped.

"You did it!" Shaundra said. "Open it now. Go *on.*"

Terri's hand was on the closed box. Her calm had vanished. "Shaundra—I'm afraid of what I'll find—"

"Terri! All this, and— Oh, well, if you don't want to go through with it, you shouldn't." She got up and checked out the window. "So put it back and forget it."

"*No.* I have to see what's inside." Without allowing herself any more time to think, she opened the box and began to go through the manila envelopes. She hardly paused to look at most things. Her father's high school diploma, an old driver's license, some letters, a pink slip indicating she'd been inoculated against polio, diphtheria, and whooping cough, report cards, but no newspaper clippings. No stories of accidents and police proceedings.

She squatted back on her heels and rested her head on her folded arms. "I am a fool."

"Terri? I thought you said you didn't have any family pictures." Shaundra pointed to one of the envelopes. It was half-filled with snapshots. She spilled the prints onto the floor. "Who are all those people?"

"I don't know." A young girl on a horse . . . three boys slouching in front of a ramshackle porch . . . an older woman with glasses . . . "Here, this one, this looks like Aunt Vivian when she was young— But I don't know who that is with her."

Shaundra looked over her shoulder. "Why'd he keep the pictures locked up?"

Terri shook her head silently. No mysteries revealed. New mysteries added to old ones. She went through the box again, slowly this time. She found a silver ring, several old coins, and a watch inscribed on the back, Richard Valenti. More papers. An outdated membership in the Automobile Club. A notice to report theft of credit cards to a toll-free number. A legal-looking document that announced the dissolution by divorce of the marriage of Kathryn Susso Mueller and Philip James Mueller.

She read this again. She saw the date, and she almost laughed. What was this? Some kind of weird Halloween joke? On the date of this so-called divorce, her mother hadn't even been alive.

"What is it?" Shaundra said. "What've you got there?" Terri handed her the paper without speaking. "I didn't know your parents were divorced."

"They weren't."

"But it says here—"

"It says wrong." Terri pointed to the date. "My mother had been dead for a year."

"That's freaky," Shaundra said. "Are you sure you know when your mother died?"

Terri jammed the envelope back into the box. How

could Shaundra ask something so stupid with such a serious expression?

"I was four years old when she died. The year of this—this *divorce,* I was five."

"Are you sure?"

"Am I sure? Do you think I'm retarded?"

"Well, maybe you got mixed up."

"I didn't get mixed up," Terri said coldly.

She closed the box and put it back on the closet shelf.

"Terri?" Shaundra said.

"What?" Something was choking her. She went into the kitchen and drank a glass of water. She had never felt so thirsty.

"Terri." Shaundra leaned against the kitchen door. "Hey, listen, I've figured it out." Her voice was very quiet. "You know what I think?"

Terri stared at the calendar hanging over the phone. It had been hanging right there when they moved into the apartment way back in August, and they'd never taken it down. She had forgotten about it, actually stopped seeing it. Now, she noticed that it was turned to the month of March, and that someone had circled the sixteenth in blue crayon. March. That was the month in which Philip and Kathryn Mueller had legally dissolved their marriage. March. That was fine. The only problem was that the year was wrong. Another little problem was that there hadn't *been* a divorce. Her father had been a widower in March of that year; her mother, if anything, a ghost. Could a ghost get a divorce?

"Terri, what I think is—I think your father lied to you."

"What are you talking about?" Terri turned on her. "He doesn't lie."

Shaundra chewed on her hair. "Well, that paper's got to be right. So your mom was living when they got the divorce—"

74

"They didn't get a divorce! Can't you get that through your head? She was killed in a car crash."

"Yeah, well—the thing is, it's pretty much like my mom's divorce paper. You see what I mean?" Shaundra peered at Terri. "It's not so awful—divorce. I mean, it *is*. It's *terrible*. But . . . it's okay that your mom and dad got a divorce. You know?"

"They didn't," Terri said. "They didn't! How could they? She was killed in a car crash one whole year before that." She bent down and petted Barkley rapidly. "I keep telling you—!"

"Well, maybe the car crash happened after the divorce. It's funny that your father didn't tell you. I mean, he did lie to you, Terri. Whatever it is about your mother, he must have lied to you," Shaundra said.

Nine

"Terr, come on, you're not even dressed." Her father glanced into her bedroom. He was wearing a plaid shirt, cords, sneakers. "We told Nancy we'd pick her up around eleven."

Terri didn't move. She was sitting on her bed, still in pajamas, chewing on a twist of red licorice.

"What did Nancy say we should bring besides hard-boiled eggs?"

She didn't answer. *You lied to me. Why?* She gave him a bright flat glance. Why had he and her mother gotten a divorce? Was there something about her mother he hadn't told her? Something bad?

Other, worse thoughts entered her mind. That he had lied about other things. Had he been the driver of the car that killed her mother?

"Daddy, you—" A chunk of licorice caught in her throat.

Looking down, she saw that she had twisted the licorice so much the palms of her hands were red.

"You better go wash," her father said, "and then move along and get dressed."

She kept looking down at her red palms and thinking of the red ink the judge had used to sign his name on the divorce paper. But maybe it was just a stamp, not a real signature. "Why didn't you tell me you and my mother got a divorce?" *There.* She had said it. She felt as if the breath had been slammed out of her.

76

Her father rolled up the window shades. One of them flapped loosely. He turned his head cautiously toward her. "Divorce? Where did you get that idea?"

"It's true," she said. "I know it's true."

He got a fork from the kitchen and began tightening the spring on the window shade roller. "Vivian," he said. "She told you something?"

"No," Terri said.

"She must have told you—"

"*No*. She wouldn't tell me anything. Neither of you would."

He checked the other window shade and began to tighten that spring, slotting it between the fork tines. Next to his mouth a muscle tightened as he tightened the spring.

"How could you get a divorce? She was dead when you got the divorce."

"How'd you get this idea? 'A' for imagination, Terri."

She hated his false hearty laugh. She hated him. Then, seeing his hands tremble as he put up the shade, she loved him and wished she had never gone into the box. The alarm clock suddenly buzzed. It was a crazy clock, always going off at the wrong time.

Phil pushed in the button. "We'll be late," he said, as if the alarm had been meant to remind them that they were going on a picnic. But neither of them moved.

"I saw the divorce paper," Terri said.

"You saw—what do you mean?" His hand went to his pocket for his key ring.

"I saw it in the box."

"The box?"

"I opened the metal box."

"You opened it?" he repeated. And again his hand went to his pocket.

"I opened it," she confirmed.

He stared at her, just stared—surprised, she felt, and hurt, as if she had betrayed him. Then she saw something else move across his face like a shadow. Fear? She wanted to shout, *Don't you be afraid!*

He walked out. She sat there, feeling stunned, numb. She had told him. Now what? Where was he going? What was he doing? She heard him in his room. Then he was back, carrying the metal box. "You opened it," he said, as if he hadn't really believed it until he saw for himself. "How?"

"I pried it open with a knife. My jackknife."

The phone rang. It rang three times, then stopped.

"You wouldn't tell me anything," she said. "I asked you to tell me. I wanted to know . . . I thought I would find out . . . find something in the box—"

"That's private," he said. "I don't see how you just did that. It's private," he repeated, as if that was the really important thing.

How could her father talk that way? Yes, she had gone into the private box, but *he* had *lied* to her. It was as if they were in a bombed-out building, but all her father would talk about was a broken window.

"If I'd wanted you to see what was in there, I would have showed you." His face looked chalky. "Couldn't you trust me?"

She felt a painful tightening under her ribs. She didn't know how to fight with her father. They never had fights. They had always seemed to naturally agree about most things. "You could have told me . . . and those pictures—why didn't you show them to me . . . *why?*" She began to cry, but when he tried to put his arm around her, she jerked away. "Don't! Leave me alone!"

They hardly spoke on the way to Nancy's house. She and Leif were waiting on the steps with a styrofoam picnic box next to them. Nancy was wearing a boy's baseball cap perched backward on her blonde hair, and a green nylon jacket with SLUGGER written on it. As soon as he saw the truck, Leif ran to the curb.

"Hi, Phil! Hi, Terri! Open up! Can I do the steering wheel?"

In the truck, Nancy leaned across Terri to kiss Phil. "Isn't it a super day for a picnic? Might be the last one of the year. I'm so glad we decided . . ." She glanced at Terri, then Phil, then Terri. "Hey, am I interrupting something?"

"Oh, Terri and I are having a small disagreement," her father said.

Terri, squeezed between her father, and Nancy and Leif, moved so no part of her touched her father. A small disagreement? He made it sound as if they were bickering over her allowance, or watching a TV show.

In the park the air was smoky and the smell of cooking meat hung over everything. It was a perfect, clear, crisp fall day. The park was filled with people. Nancy and Phil set out the food while Terri played with Leif. "Chow time," Nancy called. Everything looked good, but Terri didn't feel hungry. Not even for the German potato salad Nancy had made and which was one of her favorite foods.

"You're eating like a bird, hon," Nancy said. Her own plate was heaped with food.

Terri's father glanced at her. She looked away. She didn't look at him. She didn't want to, and she just couldn't. A red maple leaf drifted through the air and landed on the dish of hard-boiled eggs. "If that doesn't remind me of pressing leaves between waxed paper." Nancy was doing all the talking, trying hard to keep things cheerful. "Terri, you remember pressing leaves?"

"Second grade." Terri forced a smile. She had gone to school with her three big yellow tulip tree leaves and her roll of waxed paper in its long narrow blue box.

"What's this for?" her teacher had said, looking at the waxed paper.

"For the leaves. You said waxed paper."

"But, dear, I wanted you to iron them at home. Everyone did it at home. We don't have an ironing board in school."

"I know," Terri said. She and Phil didn't have an ironing board, or an iron either. Kids were laughing.

79

Terri told herself, Guess what! You did a funny thing! She laughed as loud as everyone else, covering the shame. She still hated to use waxed paper, even to wrap up a sandwich.

They finished eating, threw the paper plates into a trash basket, and sat around the table, talking. At any rate, Nancy talked. But in the middle of a story about one of her courses, she broke off to say, "You two are still mad at each other! Why don't you use me as mediator? Each tell me your side of the problem. I promise not to be prejudiced."

"Terri and I will settle it," her father said. He put his hand over Terri's. "What *are* we fighting about?" he said, not as if he didn't remember, but only as if all the heat had been over a little nothing. And for a moment, confused by the familiar warmth of his hand, Terri thought the same thing. What *are* we fighting over? Terri and Phil fighting? Unreal!

She pushed her toe deep into leaves. Her father's hand stayed on hers. Leif left the table and picked up a stick. "This is a road," he sang, dragging the stick, "this is a house, this is me. This is a truck. I'm gonna drive, gonna drive Phil's truck. Vrooom . . . vrooom . . ."

Her father's hand pressed on hers and the warmth of it crept through her. All she had to say was, We're not fighting about *anything*. Forget it . . . I was wrong . . . All she had to do was forget what she had seen . . . go back to being Daddy's good little girl . . .

She yanked her hand free. "Why did you lie to me?" she whispered tightly.

Ten

As they walked along the path, Nancy let herself lean a little against Phil. Leif, perched on Phil's shoulders, looked down at her, his face bathed in dappled light. "Hi, there," she said, squeezing her son's hand. What a shame Terri wasn't with them, that she was back at the picnic table feeling bad. Nancy, herself, felt so good she wanted everyone else to feel just as good.

"What's with Terri?" she said. "Case of adolescent sulks?" Oh, thank god, she was through that part of her life! Thank god she was past the misery of her marriage. Thank *god* she had met Phil and that he was the kind of man he was—wholeheartedly devoted to his child. "It's so unlike Terri to sulk," she went on. "Even if you did have a disagreement."

"Well . . . she's been this way all morning." Phil held Leif's ankles firmly. His voice was mild enough, but he had rarely, if ever, felt so annoyed—no, angry—with his daughter. Underneath the anger, a thread of fear moved, crawled into his gut.

"If you'd tell me what happened," Nancy said, "I'm sure I could help you two straighten it out."

"I don't think so," Phil said. What a mess that Terri had gotten into the box. Stupid of him to have hung onto the divorce certificate. He had wiped out the past with Kathryn, erased the slate clean, but kept that paper. Why? Some primitive fear of destroying documents? He mused over this idea. There were a lot of things people did that were inexplicable. Himself, included. He was an emotional, feeling person, depended on his instincts. In the long run, it was best, but sometimes it got you into a fix.

Never mind that. The question was—now what? From Terri he'd never expected anything like breaking into the box. She was such a straightforward kid. Not a sneaky bone in her body. It was overhearing that conversation he'd had with Vivian . . . it had gotten her all fevered up. Why Vivian couldn't give up playing big sister-mother to him. If only she hadn't started in on him . . .

Someday, when Terri was older, he'd tell her everything—when she could understand and appreciate what he'd done. Sometimes he imagined the telling and how she would react. Other times, he thought that he would never tell, he couldn't, it was something he'd have to keep secret for the rest of his life.

On his shoulders, Leif said, "Phil! You hurt my ankles. I'll pull your hair!"

"Sorry, sport." He loosened his grip.

Nancy put her arm through his, and he held it tight to his side. She was taller than he was, and he liked that. He liked so much about her—her spirit and her enthusiasm for life. She had had a rough time, but she hadn't been soured. Since he met her, he'd been allowing himself dreams . . . old, good dreams of a big family . . . the four of them . . . more kids . . . maybe a big old house he'd fix up . . . and laughter . . . lots of laughter . . .

Was Terri jealous of Nancy? She'd had his attention, love, devotion exclusively for so long, and he was crazy about her, had been since she was a wee baby he could hold in the palm of his hand. But lately she was different . . . not so open, not so sweet . . . Maybe he ought to talk to somebody about it, he thought with a rush of emotion, a start of tears to his eyes . . . talk about how he and Terri had been alone for so long and how much he loved her, and how carefully he had brought her up. He was so proud of her. They had been through a lot together. He had managed, no problems they couldn't handle . . . even the girl stuff. She knew she could talk to him, and she did talk to him. Her frankness and sweetness had stunned him. He was constantly amazed by his daughter.

Now the question was how to do things the best way, so no one was hurt, not Terri, and not Nancy, either . . .

As if she'd read his mind, Nancy said, "Everything seems so important when you're that age."

He looked at her. If he told her . . . did he dare? She'd understand . . . he was sure of that. Still . . . better not. "She got into some papers of mine, that's what it's all about," he said. How could something so insubstantial as a piece of paper make a difference between him and Terri? He had given up everything for her, more than she would ever know. And if he had to, he would do it again, too, in a moment, like *that*.

As they rounded the bend in the path he saw Terri still sitting at the picnic table. "Hiii!" Nancy called, waving.

"Hi," Terri said, but she didn't wave. Her throat tightened. Nancy, Leif, and her father looked perfect together.

Nancy sat down next to her and put her arm around Terri. "Your dad tells me you got into some papers of his. I'm sure there was a good reason, but if you don't speak, how can Phil know?"

Some *papers!* Terri wanted Nancy to take her arm away. She wanted to knock the glass of Cold Duck out of her father's hand. She wanted to shout at him. Why did you tell Nancy only *that?* Only part of the truth?

All the bad things that had ever happened to her— leaving so many friends, bringing the waxed paper to school, her mother being dead—all the important things and the silly things crowded into her mind. She felt tears coming. *No.* She jumped up and walked away from her father, Leif, and Nancy.

She walked past a bunch of kids playing softball. A girl in grey sweat pants ran after a boy, trying to tag him out. Terri cut through the park. She heard Nancy calling her, and kept walking. In the parking lot she thought about sitting in the truck, or maybe going into the camper and lying down, but she kept going, out of the lot and up the road.

She walked for a long time and every time a car came up behind her she'd think it was her father out looking for her. She walked into Maysville, a small town with a railroad running through the middle of it, and a bunch of bars and little stores going down a hill. Ahead, she saw a stone quarry. Where the earth had been blasted it was a grey tumble of rocks with nothing at all growing.

As she walked, she looked at everything. Nearly every house she passed she wished she could be inside and be invisible, and see the people and what they put in their houses, and the things they did, and how they talked to each other. She noticed a brick house painted yellow. A sign out front said FOR SALE . . . OPEN HOUSE. It had a side porch with white shining pillars and bunches of purple mums growing against the cellar windows. People were going in and out.

A man and a woman got out of a car and walked up the path. Terri walked behind them, and they all went inside together. A woman wearing a fur coat and orange-framed glasses greeted them. "Please sign in. Look around. I'll answer any questions." Terri walked behind the couple through the house, looking into every room, imagining the perfect family who had lived in these perfect rooms.

She got home late. The truck was parked in the lot, and there were lights on in the apartment. The stairs smelled good, the fresh, sharp smell of clean linoleum. Even before she got to the top step the door opened. "I *thought* I heard something," Nancy said, "It's her, Phil. It's *Terri*." She stood aside to let Terri in.

Her father took her arm, not gently. "Where *were*

you?" She felt the shock of his yelling at her. "We've been worried *sick*."

"You didn't have to worry." She tried to walk past him.

He held her. "What do you mean, I didn't have to worry? I can't believe this. My daughter disappears for four hours and then says I don't have to worry!"

"I can take care of myself," Terri said, stiffening her nose against the treacherous tears.

"Don't be stupid, please. That is not you talking. When have you ever gone away for four hours?" His eyes were bright, his voice shaking. "I think you owe Nancy an apology. Nancy and me, because we've both been out of our minds."

"Apologize?" Terri said. "You should apologize to me, Daddy. You didn't tell me the truth. *Why didn't you tell me the truth?*" The sound of her voice was strange in her ears. She sounded far away, creaking, like an old gate. She thought someone was crying. In a moment she realized it was herself. She was crying . . . that creaking crying sound was her. And her father was crying, too.

Eleven

In Terri's mind what happened that Sunday evening in their house with her father was never entirely clear. That is, the sequence of events was unclear—it was like being in an accident and, afterward, remembering only the sight of the other car coming straight for you —the moment of impact forever a blank.

And, afterward, too, there was that curious numbness that comes with an accident. A lack of feeling, a lack of connection, all the nerve endings frozen, so that the little shocks you expect as you remember the accident don't come. They hit the frozen nerves and are stopped dead. Then you go through the day after the accident, smiling and talking and thinking, *I'm normal. I'm unaffected*. Only later, much later, do you find the bruises, and discover that you ache everywhere.

Overnight, the weather changed. The morning sky was low, full of heavy grey clouds. Wet black leaves fell from the trees. As Terri walked into school she noticed with a feeling of surprise that everything was the way it always was. The halls were crowded. Boys were sitting on the trophy case near the gym. Couples holding hands and patting each other lined the second-floor landing near the window. How could everything be exactly as it was before when, for her, nothing would ever be the same again?

First they had cried. Don't ever do that to me again,

he said. You have to tell me, she said. Tell me the truth . . .

Leif was playing with pots and pans, banging them together.

You and my mother were divorced. Is that right? That's what the paper said.

He nodded. Yes.

A divorce? Nancy said. She still had the baseball cap on her head. A divorce? Phil . . . I thought . . . I don't understand . . .

It's a very hard thing to talk about, he said. If Terri hadn't found the divorce decree . . .

She walked to her locker, carrying with her, like something tangible, that curious numbness, that detachment. She saw little details with extraordinary clarity. A sharp-nosed girl wearing a fluffy white fur hat with earflaps. A boy with slicked-back blond hair, each hair lying separate and distinct on his head. And the smells of the school—Lysol, oregano (pizza for lunch again), and cigarette smoke—came to her in parallel waves, so that she smelled them all at once, and yet individually.

He wiped his eyes. Terri, can't you take me on faith? All these years . . . let it drop now, Terri . . . Pleading. You found something . . . you opened a can of worms . . .

Divorce? Nancy said.

He walked up and down the room, clasping his crossed arms. Yes. Kathryn and I were divorced. Yes. A rumpled, sleepy look on his face. Yes. Now you know. Okay? Is that it?

Divorce? Nancy said.

He didn't look at her. He looked at Terri. All right? Now you have the truth.

But . . . but . . . there's more, she said.

More?

Isn't there? She knew there was. She saw that in the way he looked at her. In the way he didn't look at her.

In the way he went to the window, turned his back on her. The silence was long. Nancy broke it.

More? Nancy said. Is there more, Phil?

Yes. His voice was muffled. Terri felt a wave of hard pity in her chest. Her heart beat in slow, heavy strokes. She thought her heart beat like the strokes of an old clock.

I don't want to tell you, he said. I don't want to tell you. It's up to you, Terri. It's up to Terri. We can stop this right now. We can just forget it . . . go back to the way things were . . .

She had come dutifully to school. She went dutifully to each class, her feet taking her automatically. She sat in her seat; she opened her notebook; she took out her Bic pen. Perhaps she even wrote down things that made sense. She copied assignments. She looked seriously at her teachers, and listened to other kids talking. Once someone made a joke and everyone laughed. She laughed, too.

The whole morning passed in this way: sharp moments of sight and sound, then a blurred rush of time. In her head the voices of last night whispered sharply. Outside, it was raining. The windows were streaked, the lights on. Inside, the school was crowded, warm, steamy; it was like a cave. She saw them all, students and teachers, strange beasts rushing from den to den, huddling together. In the hall she liked being jostled. If someone pushed her she would welcome it—hands pushing her, shoving her forward, because her feet moved so slowly, stumblingly.

In English Mr. Higgens gave one of his surprise quizzes. He roamed the aisles, his fierce popping eyes keeping everyone in line. No cheating in his class! "Terri—" Mr. Higgens was standing over her, gazing at her nearly blank test paper. "Do you plan to finish?" She nodded. "Terrific. You have eight minutes."

She bent over the paper. . . . The bell rang. She had written nothing, been unaware of the time passing. She put the paper on Mr. Higgens' desk. He glanced at it.

"Wait a minute, Terri." The room emptied. "Well, what is it?" he said. "What's going on with you? You're a pretty girl. Do you expect to be passed on your looks? Eh? Eh?"

She shook her head.

"Were you thinking about English? Or were you thinking about your boyfriend?"

"No."

"No? I get up here every day and try to teach you kids some respect for the English language. Do you realize you're going to be handicapped in life unless you learn what I've got to teach you? Handicapped!" He took her test paper and hurled it to the floor.

She didn't want to cry.

Mr. Higgens leaped out of his seat, his face working. "What are you crying for? You silly girl!" He patted her head vigorously. "Don't you know by now I only mean a quarter of what I say?"

His face swam in front of her, those big popping eyes . . . Was he feeling sorry for her? He didn't know. How could he? No one knew but her and her father and Nancy.

"Good lord, girl! Here, have a tissue." He dumped a box of tissues in front of her, then flung himself back into his chair. "You kids will make a nervous wreck of me yet."

He said it seriously, as if he was the World's Calmest Person, being driven over the edge by his students. Laughter tore at her throat.

"Terri—" His eyes popped. "If you need someone to talk to, I'm here."

"Thank you," she said. She wanted to say more, wanted to tell him he was kind and she liked him. "Can I have a pass to my next class?"

He wrote it out. "See you tomorrow. I hope we're both in better shape."

In the hall she saw Shaundra. "Hi!" Shaundra caught her arm. She was wearing high-waisted jeans with black and orange suspenders. "Where you going?"

"Class. I was just talking to Mr. Higgens." Amazing that she sounded so normal.

"Meet me after school. I gotta rush now, library pass."

The afternoon went by in fits and starts. Voices had an odd hollow quality. And words—words fit together in a recognizable way, but the sense was hard to catch. Sometimes, lost in her thoughts, she heard nothing.

Her father sighed, sighed again and again, as if he had trouble getting enough air. And, later, he cried again. And, later, she said to Nancy, No! Leave him alone! But that was later, and by then they had talked for hours, and she was tired, so tired . . .

Could she talk to Shaundra about it? Maybe she would never tell anyone. She caught a glimpse of herself in a window. A tall girl with a braid down her back, wearing jeans, a blue Ivy shirt, a gold chain, a short white sweater with just the bottom button done up. She didn't look different, or strange. Could anyone tell?

Shaundra was waiting for her near the front doors. It was raining, thick grey sheets of rain. "Whose house should we go to?" Shaundra put her books over her head.

"Yours." They walked through puddles. Soggy leaves filled the gutters.

Well, what happened after the divorce, Phil? Nancy said. Did you get custody of Terri?

No, I didn't get anything.

Her mother had custody? And then, after the car accident, you—

There was no car accident.

There was no car accident?

There was no car accident.

No car accident . . . no car accident . . . no car accident. . . no car accident . . .

"My mother *told* me to take an umbrella," Shaundra said. "She said it was going to rain. I hate it when my mother is right."

I'm confused, Phil. If there was no car accident . . .

90

Nancy sat on the edge of the couch. *For the first time Terri noticed how lumpy it was and that pieces of stuffing were coming out of the arms. She hated that couch. Until that moment she didn't know she hated it.*

"Did Higgens give your class a quiz today?"

"Yes."

"Us, too! How'd you do?"

"I don't know. Not good."

"Oh, I bet you did fine. You're so smart. *I* probably flunked!"

Then how did Kathryn die, Phil?

She didn't die.

She didn't—you mean— Is she alive?

Yes. As far as I know.

Terri's mother is alive? Where is she? Where is Terri's mother, Phil?

Oh, god, can we stop this? Can we stop this interrogation? Terri—I did it for you. They were going to take you away.

Did what, Phil? You did what?

Must I? he said. Must I tell you?

"You know what I just thought of," Saundra said.

"What?"

"You know! What we did on Friday."

"Friday?"

"Terri! Stop teasing me! The box. Your father's box."

He pushed up the sleeves of his shirt. The lines around his mouth were drawn deep, yet there was a curious half smile on his lips. Terri recognized that smile—the crocodile smile, the smile that you can't control. The smile that doesn't belong on your face, but there it is. She had felt that smile coming over her once when a boy in her fifth grade class fell down and hit his head against the metal leg of a chair. He bled. Looking at him, white on the floor, before she understood it was terrible, or maybe just as she understood, she smiled. She had put her hand to her mouth to hide that awful smile.

"Did you tell your father?" Shaundra said. "Did you tell him about the box? What you did?"

Terri blinked, her heart jumped—a sign of life in the cold. *Friday* when she broke open the box? Only Friday? It seemed so long ago. Much, much longer than two days ago. Much, much longer than the day before the day before yesterday.

Must I? he said. He appealed to her. Terri— she felt small and weak. She leaned against the wall. Terri, we can just forget it . . . just let it drop . . . We're happy . . . It's up to you, he said. You say the word, Terri. You tell me, Okay, Daddy, you've gone far enough. You say it, Terri.

"I told him," she said.

"You did! Did you mention me?" Shaundra clutched Terri's arm. "You have so much nerve." She shuddered dramatically. Her bunny fur jacket was slick with rain. "You said you would, but I didn't think you really would!"

She had wanted to say, Yes, Daddy, yes, let's go back to where we were . . . before Aunt Vivian came . . . before I heard you talking . . . before I opened the box . . . back . . . back . . . it was safe back there . . . safe . . .

She said, I want to know, Daddy. I want to know it all.

"Well, what happened? Was he *furious?* What about the other thing—you know, the divorce, and— Are you still mad at me for saying he lied to you?"

"But he did," Terri said. Her voice sounded small, choked.

"Oh, Terri—*why?*"

"Please, Shaundra—I don't want to talk about it right now."

"I understand." Shaundra squeezed her arm consolingly.

I was left with nothing, he said. No home. No wife. No child. Kathryn was going to get married again.

*Clem. Clem Bradshaw. And Terri began to call him
Daddy Clem.*

"Oh, this rain," Shaundra said. "I'm soaked. Well,
semi-soaked, pretty soon I'll be totally soaked. I wish
we had a ride. We should hitch a ride. You want to
hitch a ride? Would you *dare?*"

"All right," Terri said.

"You would do it?"

"Why not?" Terri felt again that blankness, that
nothingness. She was wet and chilled, and all that was
trivial.

*Maybe, he said, Terri wouldn't have forgotten me
altogether, but it would never have been the same. He'd
be with her all the time, this other guy, this man—
Clem— He'd be there when she had something to tell
. . . he'd be there when she was sick, he'd be there,
all the time . . .*

"Oh, you wouldn't hitch. You're just saying that.
What if somebody picked us *up?*"

"That's the point, isn't it?" Terri stepped into the
road and stuck out her thumb.

"Terri, you nut!"

A car passed. "You're the one who wanted to do it."

"I've never hitched a ride! Have you?"

"No." Terri kept her thumb up. The driver of another car looked at her, but didn't slow down. Her
heart seemed to race along with the car, speeding,
speeding. She felt calm, reckless, strangely adrift.

*Then it turned out they were going to move out of
the country. He lined up a job teaching in a school in
Italy. In Milan. The American School in Milan. One
day when I came for Terri, I saw a letter addressed to
him. He and Kathryn must have been talking about it,
and he left the letter. I saw the return address. The
American School, Via Bezzola, Milano. I never forgot
that. Via Bezzola. That's when it became real to me,
and I knew I couldn't let them, couldn't let her . . .*

Shaundra pulled at Terri's arm. "Come *on!* You're

weird today. You're supposed to have *sense*, of the two of us."

"One more car." She walked backward, thumb out. It didn't matter. It didn't matter. Nothing was what it seemed. Strangely, just then she remembered Sally the Mouse and Mustafa riding off in their Mousemobile.

The next visiting day I was ready. We left. I drove all day, we slept by the road that night, drove again the next day. She was good. I gave her orange soda and half a tranquilizer, to be sure. We sang songs. Played games. After a while I told her about Kathryn . . .

Words, Terri thought. Words. For a moment she felt hard, bright, and solid, like a piece of metal. All the words her father had said reverberated in her mind, clanged against that metal.

"Holy schlamoly!" Shaundra grabbed Terri's arm. A car slowed down. Two boys in the front seat grinned at them. The boy nearest Terri had a long narrow head, a long thin nose, wise and sly, pretty blue eyes. "Want a ride?"

"Yes," Terri said. She got in the car. Shaundra gasped, then, muttering, followed her.

Both boys turned around. The other boy, the driver, was dark-eyed, had a crew cut, the beginnings of a mustache.

"Hi!" he said.

"Hi," Shaundra said.

"You're cute. How old are you?"

"None of your beez-niss, meester." Shaundra had recovered. She leaned toward Terri. "I didn't think you would really do it," she whispered.

"Come on, how old are you girls, really?" The car glided away from the curb.

"Old enough to know better," Shaundra said.

"I bet you're under age."

"I bet you are, too!"

The boys laughed. "What's your name?" the driver asked, looking in the rearview mirror.

"Me to know, you to guess. What's yours?"

"I'm Sonny."

"Oh, Sonny Boy," Shaundra sang, bouncing a little on the seat next to Terri.

"You can trust a boy with the name Sonny," he said. "My friend's name is Jim."

"*Slim* Jim," Shaundra said.

Jim couldn't control his laughter. He kept breaking into high-pitched giggles.

Terri stared out the window. She heard Shaundra and the boys bantering back and forth. She said nothing. How stupid, she thought. How very dumb. Why did I do this? It was senseless, as senseless as what her father had confessed. And it all came back to her again, the words, and the sense of the words, pouring down on her like water, like the grey rain falling in straight sheets out of the sky.

She cried some in the beginning. Nights, she cried, and I rocked her in my lap.

What you're saying, Phil . . . You're saying you kidnapped her. You kidnapped your own daughter. My god, Phil, my god.

I don't think you should say that. I took her. I just took her. All I did was take her, take what was mine . . .

Yours? You kidnapped her.

Then he cried.

Then she said, Leave him alone. Nancy, leave him alone, can't you? Just leave him alone!

"Where should we go?" Sonny said.

"Not far," Shaundra said. "You can let us out at the next corner."

"What? Oh, no! Don't be a party pooper. Let's go for a ride."

"Okay, a ride to my house," Shaundra directed. "It's on Millson Street."

"Millson Street? Okay, okay. But you gotta tell me your name."

"Well . . . maybe I will, and maybe I won't . . ."

"That's not fair. I told you my name. I told you my friend's name. Sonny and Jim. And you're—"

"Oh, okay. Shaundra."

"Shaundra. Great! What's your silent friend's name? What's her name? Hey, you, back there, what's your name?"

Terri stared out the window. It was raining, raining, a hard grey rain.

Kidnapped. Kidnapped? Kidnapped your own daughter. Kidnapped by her father. Silly! Made no sense. Kidnappers were sinister men, ugly men, violent men. Kidnappers had cut off a boy's ear and sent it to his family. This was to prove they would do what they said if they didn't get their money. Money was what kidnappers cared about . . .

Shaundra tugged her arm. "Tell them your name." What if Sonny drove past Shaundra's house, out of the city, into the country, onto a back road . . . She felt a little stab of fear in her belly and welcomed it. A feeling. She had been numb for so many hours. She leaned forward.

"My name is Terri Mueller." And in her head she heard her voice continuing, *And my mother isn't dead after all.* She heard this so distinctly it surprised her that no one reacted.

"Terri and Shaundra. Nice. Where do you girls go to school?"

"Where do you boys go to school?" Shaundra countered.

"Do you answer every question with a question?"

"Do you? Turn here," she instructed.

"What if I don't?"

"I scream." The boys laughed. They were in the middle of a long line of cars. "Here, right here! That's my corner."

Sonny kept driving.

Shaundra screamed.

"Hey!" He swiveled his head. The car rocked. "Don't do that!"

"I want to get out!" Shaundra put her hand on the door handle. "Let's go, Terri!"

The car went through an intersection, picked up speed. "What's the matter, your mamas won't let you take a ride?"

Shaundra opened the door. The blue-eyed Jim gaped, mouth open. The pavement whizzed by below the half-opened door. "Is she crazy?" Jim asked Terri.

"Yeah, I'm *crazy*. I'm a real maniac and you better let me out." Shaundra gave another long piercing scream. "I drink blood!" she yelled.

The boys looked at each other. There was a stop sign ahead, a cluster of stores, and gas stations on the four corners. The car rolled to a stop. Shaundra and Terri scrambled out.

"Chicken," Sonny said, sticking his head out the window.

The girls ran back toward Shaundra's house. They couldn't stop laughing. Terri laughed so hard she felt sick to her stomach, laughed so hard she cried. Cried and laughed, and couldn't tell where her laughter ended and her tears began.

Twelve

Phil didn't sleep well again Monday night. Again he had many dreams. In one dream he saw a bejeweled train in the distance, like a fabulous child's toy. Crying out with wonder, he called Terri to come and look. "You see," he said to her, loving her greatly, "you see how it is!"

In his dreams, also, his former wife came back. She was striding down a street, yellow-tinted sunglasses up on her forehead, holding a Japanese vegetable knife in her hand. "You'd better hurry, Phil," she said authoritatively, and he felt his anger at her harden like a stone in his heart. This anger woke him. In the bare darkened room, he stared at the ceiling and thought that the woman in his dream actually had not looked at all like Kathryn.

He glanced at the clock. Time to get up. He felt very tired and thought that it would be nice not to go to work. But then what? In the other room he heard the dog's toenails click on the floor. He heard Terri moving around. "Good morning," he called. She didn't answer.

She didn't hear me, he told himself. He dressed, laced up his boots, noticing that they needed a shine. Fleetingly he wished their apartment were nicer. He put keys and money in his pocket, then his wallet, first glancing at Nancy's picture. Very glamorous, her hair whipping out behind her, a big white glistening smile. A picture to impress. He knew her better. The real Nancy was soft, giving, needing.

He thought of Sunday afternoon when Terri had disappeared for so many hours . . . And then her return. He thought of it rapidly, feeling somehow damaged, but also with a curious relief and emptiness. The phrase *the dirty little secret* came to mind. He yawned with that empty feeling and pulled up the shade. It had snowed overnight. The roofs were frosted with white. The first snow of the season. Going to his closet for a heavier jacket, he told himself that Terri's insistence on knowing the truth reflected well on him. She had a mind, and spirit, too. This was the way he had brought her up. He would match her against any girl her age.

"It snowed, Terr," he said, walking into the kitchen. He kissed her on the cheek. "Good morning," he said again, and was surprised by an exquisite sense of relief when she replied, "Good morning, Daddy," then turned, as on any other morning, to fill the coffeepot for him.

After the coffee, she cracked eggs into the poacher. Barkley was at the window, nose pressed to glass, whining excitedly at the sight of snow. Her father began their lunches. He was wearing a dark green plaid shirt, denims; his eyes were a little puffy. She felt that he looked at her uneasily. She felt sleepy herself, dream-filled; she was in a little trance.

She dropped slices of bread into the toaster, set out plates, silverware, napkins. They never rushed through breakfast. Her father wrapped peanut butter sandwiches, yawned, licked his fingers. Yes, he was definitely avoiding her eyes. It was Tuesday morning, and they had not really talked since Sunday night. She moved around in an orderly way, quietly, not quite connected. Gradually, slowly, she had realized something —her mother had not died. She had a mother.

Waking, she had said it out loud. "I have a mother." The words were shocking. Something seemed to burst in her mind.

She sat down across from her father. She'd left the eggs in the poacher too long, and the yellow centers were hard. She poked at her egg. Was her mother sitting at a table now? Did she like eggs? Was she a morning person? *A tall, handsome woman.* Sipping her milk, Terri mused over her aunt's words. A tall, handsome woman would be a strong woman, someone you could respect and admire. She strained to make it seem real.

"There are a lot of things you haven't told me," she said abruptly to her father.

He poured coffee, his thumb over the little glass ball in the center of the pot cover. "Such as?"

"Why did you and my mother get divorced?"

"A long complicated story. I'm not sure I remember that well anymore, Terri. It was a long time ago . . ."

"Did you fight?"

"Well, sure."

"What'd you fight over?"

"Is this what we're going to talk about for breakfast from now on?" He took money out of his pocket. "We need cheese and butter. Will you pick it up after school?"

He looked sad and uncomfortable and it was too hard for her to keep pressing. She took the money and put it in her back pocket.

But later, after he'd gone and just before she went to school, she saw a workshirt of his on the bathroom floor near the green wicker hamper. Ordinarily she would have picked up the shirt, dropped it in the hamper. Now she didn't want to touch it. She toed the shirt into a corner, shoved it out of sight.

The sun came out as she walked to school. She pulled off her white Icelandic wool hat. She had also worn wool mittens, her down vest. They had bought them all through the Bean catalogue in the fall, marking the items together, also ordering a Bean shirt and flannel pajamas for her father.

100

At the corner near the school she saw Shaundra and George Torrance talking. "Hi-iii!" Shaundra waved. Terri's legs stiffened. Did she have to walk straight toward them? Why did she still feel this way about George? She wasn't even sure she liked him, although she couldn't find anything wrong with him. But then she had hardly ever really talked to him.

"Hi." She knew her face was red.

"Hi-iiii!" Shaundra said.

"Hi," George mumbled. His eyes were down. His eyes were always down. Didn't he want to look at her?

"We were just talking about ice skating," Shaundra said. "We were just saying maybe we'd all go ice skating some afternoon this winter."

George was wearing an oversize purple sweater covered with polka dots. An ugly sweater. Terri didn't like the way he dressed. She sighed softly as they walked up the steps to school. The good thing about being near George was that she found it impossible to think about anything else.

At the top of the stairs, George rushed to open the door for her and Shaundra. "You don't have to do that," Terri said.

"Why not?" He held the door for Shaundra.

"It's— I'm not *helpless.*"

"I didn't say— She doesn't want me to open the door for her," George said to Shaundra.

"Oh, she's crazy, anyway," Shaundra said. "She really is." Her voice was excited and gay. They walked toward their lockers. "You know what this crazy girl did?"

Terri turned her head. *Oh, no.* Was Shaundra going to tell about the hitchhiking?

"She broke open a *locked* box of her father's!"

Terri couldn't believe Shaundra had said that. Worse, *worse,* than talking about picking up those boys.

"A locked box?" George said. "What was in it?"

Terri threw her lunch into her locker and rushed

down the hall. Shaundra came after her. "Terri, hey, Terri—"

"Why'd you say that? Why did you?"

"I don't know," Shaundra said. Her frizzy dark hair fell around her face. Her eyes peeped out. "I wasn't thinking, I guess, it just came out . . . you know. You're always so quiet around George. I was just trying to show him that you're really lively and fun and—"

"You shouldn't have said that!"

"Well, maybe I wouldn't have, if you'd told me what happened. I asked you yesterday."

What was she supposed to tell Shaundra? *Oh, yeah, it turns out that I was kidnapped. It was my father who did it. By the way, another interesting tidbit is that my mother never was in that car accident. Yeah, she's not dead.*

"It's—it's private," Terri said.

"It wasn't too private for me to be right there when you did it."

"That was different."

"I don't see how."

"Shaundra, can we just drop this? This isn't the place to talk about it."

"Nobody will hear."

A couple wearing identical tight blue Levi's passed, their hands in each other's back pockets. "There are people all around," Terri said.

"Sure!" Shaundra dug her hands into her hair. "I get it now, Terri. You don't *trust* me. That's why you won't tell me—you just don't plain trust me."

"Shaundra, I trust you—"

"Oh, my foot!" Shaundra said. She walked away.

Later, between classes, Terri passed Shaundra in the hall. Shaundra stuck her chin into the air, and that was that.

At lunch hour, Terri took her food outside. The sun had come out, and the snow was gone. Terri leaned against the building and slowly ate her peanut butter sandwich. A feeling of total misery gripped her. She had quarreled with Shaundra, and she didn't know what to think about her father. She had been so proud of their life together, of him, of the deep, close love they shared. But it had been built on lies.

She walked home after school trying to think only about a composition she had to write for English and something good to eat for supper. Around the corner from her house, she shopped in Azria's Groceteria, adding chocolate chip cookies and maple walnut ice cream to the morning list.

Outside Azria's there was a dilapidated phone booth. When they'd first moved here, before their phone was installed, they'd used this one. Now, just as she walked by, the phone rang. That shrill sound in the empty booth gave her the most terrible feeling. At the other end of the line, someone was waiting for someone else to pick up the receiver. A someone else who would never answer.

The phone rang again. My mother, she thought. What if that's my mother? She stepped into the booth. "Hello?" she said, picking up the receiver.

"Hello," a man said. "Is Frank there? Frank the plumber?"

Terri stared at the debris on the floor, an oily rag in one corner, scraps of wet paper. Telephone numbers and names were scrawled on the walls, and just above the phone someone had written SOLAR POWER TO THE PEOPLE, enclosing the words in a red circle with red sun rays streaming out of it.

"Hello!" he said.

"This is a phone booth," she said finally.

"Wrong number, I guess." He hung up.

Terri didn't move. *My mother,* she thought again. *I have a mother. She is somewhere in this world. At this very moment* . . . Was she talking on her phone? Buying milk and eggs? Tying her shoelaces, or petting a cat, or eating a piece of toast? The small realness of all this made Terri dizzy. She leaned back against the cold glass.

I have to find her, she thought, and then, foolishly, scoffing at herself, but stubbornly unreasonable, she stayed in the booth waiting for the phone to ring once more.

Thirteen

A sentence is spoken. Or thought. *I must find her.* It sinks into the mind. It sinks out of sight, but is not forgotten. Four words. *I must find her.* Her. Terri's mother. Stranger. Unknown Person. There had been Sally the Mouse and Mustafa the Mouse and now there was . . . Madame X. Mouse X. Her mother, a woman Terri had not seen for eight years. Almost two-thirds of her life.

To say is not to do. But to say is to set something in motion. *I must find her.* An urgency there, a promise Terri made to herself. But how to keep that promise? She knew so little—first name, Kathryn. Last name—Mueller? Bradshaw? Susso? With words her father had killed off her mother, so that now Kathryn Susso Mueller was only a shadow of a memory of a memory. Was this shadow, this mother, still in Oakland, California? Waiting? Waiting for Terri to return? *Bye, Mommy, see you later. I'm going with Daddy for a little ride . . .*

She made a plan. Call Oakland information. Ask for Kathryn Mueller, or Susso, or Bradshaw. Take down all the numbers. (Surely, there'd be more than one?) Call all numbers. Not much of a plan, but, nevertheless, something. A step. A beginning of keeping her promise to herself.

That night she heard her father talking on the phone to Nancy. She heard his voice, agitated, full of feeling. "I *know* it's a shock for you, but . . . I'm still the same man! Why not, Nancy? Why not? Nothing has changed—"

Then he listened for a long time. And Terri understood that they were talking about her, her "kidnapping."

When her father spoke again, it was in a soft and pleading voice. "Yes, you're right—from my point of view, it's still true. I believe in what I did. That's what this whole thing is about. Devotion to Terri. Why are you ready to hang me because I put her first?"

And again he listened. "So Kathryn is to be canonized now?" And then, "Well . . . where does that leave us? . . . What? . . . That's *nowhere* . . . All right, then . . . I can't beg you. When you're ready, you call me." He hung up.

Terri went into the kitchen. He was standing with his hand on the phone. Hearing her, he straightened up. "What's—what did Nancy say?" she asked.

."Oh . . ." He half shrugged. "She doesn't want to see me for a while. Thinks I'm a pretty bad, low-down guy for what I did." He took Barkley's leash off the hook. "I think I'll go out for a walk."

After he left she sat over her empty sheet of paper with the heading, "English, Mr. Higgens." Her fault Nancy and her father were fighting. Her fault Nancy wouldn't see him. Her fault he was unhappy.

She had said, *I must find her,* but when she passed the phone booth outside Azria's the next day she thought of Nancy and her father and kept walking.

In the bus Terri sat by a window. People were getting on in groups and pairs. She tried to look alert and happy, as if she expected someone to sit down next to her any moment. Life without a special friend was not good. She missed Shaundra. They hadn't spoken in two days; she didn't even know if Shaundra was going on the field trip to the science museum. Nobody is speaking to anybody, she thought.

Just then Naomi Willer, a big, friendly-looking girl

106

with pink cheeks, sat down next to her. "Hi, anybody sitting here?"

"You are," Terri said.

Naomi smiled. "Isn't this neat, getting out of school for the afternoon? You're in my math class, I think."

"I sit in the back," Terri said.

"How'd you do on that last test?"

"All right—well, not too good."

A few minutes later, Shaundra got on the bus. She had her hands in the pockets of her bunny fur jacket and wore a red beret perched on her mass of hair. Seeing Terri, Shaundra looked away and sat down across the aisle near the front.

"I was so glad when it snowed the other day," Naomi said. "I was hoping it would really pile up. I love winter."

George appeared with a group of other kids. "George!" Shaundra tugged at one end of the long striped scarf he wore around his neck. "You have to sit down here," she cried. Was this all for Terri's benefit? George sat down, hadn't even looked her way.

"I bet you're a skier," Terri said, stretching out a smile.

"My mother taught me when I was five. Couldn't keep me off the slopes after that. My whole family skis."

"How many of you are there?"

"Six. I'm the youngest. Three older sisters. My father is the greatest skier—no, no, I take that back. My mother is. She was almost in the winter Olympics one year. She just missed qualifying."

"Really! You must be so proud." She kept smiling, but didn't have her heart in this conversation. What would Naomi Willer, this nice girl with the braces and pink cheeks and a regular father and mother—what would this so-normal Naomi think if Terri were to say, "The year your mother was teaching you to ski, I was being kidnapped by my father"?

But what she wanted to say even more, ached to say,

was, "Look, I have a mother, also. You're not the only one!"

"Terri Mueller to the office, please." The call came over the intercom in English class. Everyone looked at her. "Terri Mueller." An urgency to the voice. Mr. Higgens grinned furiously.

"Go on, go on, nothing we can do about it."

She went slowly down the stairs. Only once before had she ever been called to the office in the middle of a school day. Three years ago, her father, working on a construction crew laying new floors in a factory, had cut straight across the palm of his hand and fore-finger with a power saw. In the emergency room, he had not forgotten Terri. Someone had called her school to let her know that he would be home late. She had never forgotten the sight of him walking into the apart-ment that night, with a jaunty, white-faced grin, and a blood-soaked bandage covering his raised hand. There was a scar across his palm still and that finger was always a little stiff and cold, especially in winter.

She opened the office door and saw the back of a tall woman in a tweed jacket standing at the counter. My mother, she thought. Of course, she's found me.

The woman turned, and it was Nancy. "Oh, Terri, there you are."

Terri felt confused and backed out. Nancy followed her. "How are you?" She hugged Terri. "Let me *look* at you!"

"I'm fine," Terri said. She almost laughed. Nancy was so extravagant. It was only a week since they'd seen each other.

"No, how are you, really?" Nancy pulled at the string of big blue beads around her neck. "I haven't been able to get you off my mind."

They moved into a corner of the hall, near the stairs. "Why—why did you come here?" Terri asked. Maybe something *had* happened to her father.

"I wanted to see you. I just wanted to see you."

Nancy tugged gently at Terri's braid. "I was on my way to the library to study, but you've been on my mind so much—did I take you away from an important class?"

"No, it's okay. Mr. Higgens had a fit, but—"

"Ahhh . . ." Nancy smiled faintly. She wasn't listening. "You see, I don't want to come to the house right now. I need time to think—about Phil and me. It's broken me up—what Phil did. I can't really take it in." Her nose reddened with emotion. "If Leif's father took him away—! It's such a terrible thought I can't even deal with it."

The bell clanged. Doors burst open, the hall and stairs filled with kids. "And I'm so angry," Nancy went on. "Angry at Phil for you . . . and for *me*. Terri, I feel betrayed."

Terri stood stiffly. What did Nancy want her to say? She wasn't going to tear down her father. She thought how everyone was choosing sides. Why did it have to be that way?

"I'm a *mother*," Nancy said. "I tried to tell Phil—"

Terri saw Shaundra and George walking down the stairs toward them. This was the worst possible place to discuss anything private, especially *that*.

"He doesn't understand, but you—"

"Nancy—" She moved, wanted to avoid Shaundra, but it was too late. George saw her, too, plucked at his watchband. Terri leaned back against the wall. "Hi." She put her hands in her back pockets, slouching. See, totally at ease.

"Hi . . . uh . . . Terri," George said with a dumb funny grin, as if he'd forgotten her name. There was almost a smile on Shaundra's round face. She and George were at the bottom of the stairs. Was the smile for Terri or for George? Should she smile back? Should she introduce Nancy? She felt her eyes twitching with strain.

"Hi," Shaundra said, not exactly speaking to Terri, but more to the wall to the right of her. And they walked on by, Shaundra bouncing and bobbing in her cute, tight-fitting jeans, and George with his red forehead and simpleton's grin.

"Friends?" Nancy said.

"Sort of."

"Terri—have you done anything yet?"

"Done anything?" Terri repeated.

"About your mother. Do you know where she lives?"

"Maybe in Oakland."

"You're not sure?" Terri shook her head. "You're going to find out, aren't you?" Nancy said. "I mean, my god, you have to, Terri. Have you talked to your father?"

"We talk. We talk all the time." Deliberately she gave Nancy a blank look, was obtuse and proud.

Nancy caught it, of course. "Terri—dear Terri—I *care* for you," she said. "I *know* you and Phil talk. I *know* how you close you two are. Surely you've talked about the kidnapping—"

"Nancy!" Her voice shot out in alarm. She looked around, pressed her fingers to her lips.

"It's nothing to be ashamed of—Ah, god, that poor woman, Terri." Nancy leaned toward her, her hair swinging over her face. "Terri," she said quietly, "you must let your mother know you're here. That you're alive." She stroked Terri's shoulder. "You have to, you know."

Terri felt a slow sinking. Nancy's brown eyes . . . yes, she was a mother . . . and she understood Terri . . . she understood that Terri couldn't hurt her father . . . and she understood, as well, how Terri longed and longed for her unknown mother . . .

"Do it," Nancy said. "Just go ahead and do it, Terri dear."

110

Fourteen

"What city?" the operator asked.

"Oakland." Terri looked out through the smudged glass at the Azria's Groceteria sign swinging in the wind. It was a chilly afternoon.

"What name?"

"Kathryn Mueller."

"M-u-l-l-e-r?"

"No. M-u-*e*-l-l-e-r."

"Address?"

"I don't know it, operator."

Kathryn Mueller? This is your daughter, Terri.

Who?

Terri.

I don't know any Terri.

If she had an address, she could write a letter. *Dear Mother* . . . Or, maybe, *Dear Kathryn, let me introduce myself. I am your daughter* . . .

Dear Kathryn, eight years ago . . .

"I have no Katherine Muellers," the operator said.

"Operator, it's not Kath-er-ine. It's Kathryn. K-a-t-h-r-y-n."

"Sorry. No Kathryn K-a-t-h-r-y-n Mueller M-u-e-l-l-e-r."

"Is there anything for Kathryn Susso, or Kathryn Bradshaw?"

"One moment please . . . No Kathryn Susso or Kathryn Bradshaw listed in Oakland."

111

"Operator, please, could you try those names with the initial K?" She couldn't give up.

"M'am, I do have one K. Mueller."

Terri scribbled down the number. It was nearly four o'clock. Maybe she should go home, start supper, do the call tomorrow morning. *Coward.* Yes, she was scared, felt that pounding in her stomach. She dialed, fumbled the numbers, had to start all over. She dropped in coins, listening to them clink into place. She could still hang up, do this some other time.

The phone barely rang once and was picked up. "Now, look, Jaime," a woman's voice said, "I told you, forget it. I've had it with you, and I mean it."

"Excuse me," Terri broke in, "I'm calling from Michigan—"

"Michigan? Who is this?"

"This is Terri—"

"Terri? Terri who?"

She could hardly speak. It was exactly as bad as she had imagined. "Terri Mueller."

"I can't hear you. Speak up, please."

"Terri Mueller." She forced out her voice. "Is this Kathryn Mueller?"

"This is Kris. Who is this, anyway?"

"I'm looking for Kathryn Mueller who had a child—"

"Wait a second, wait a second. I don't have a child, and believe me, I don't plan to. Is this some warped joke of Jaime's? I bet it is. Listen, will you give Jaime a message for me? *So long, Jaime!"* She hung up.

"I called California today," Terri said. Her father looked up with a mouthful of ice cream. "Oakland. I got the number of K. Mueller from the operator, and I called after school." It was too bad the way her heart was pulsing. "I thought K. Mueller might be my mother."

He put down his spoon. "Was it?"

112

"No." Her braid swung over one shoulder. "I tried Kathryn Susso, too, and Kathryn Bradshaw."

"Busy, weren't you?" he said.

Sarcasm? She wasn't used to that from him. But then, this was a whole new world. "I want to talk to my mother," she said. She bent to stroke Barkley. "Does Aunt Vivian know where my mother is?"

"Possibly." Oh, Terri. He wanted to plead with her. "You won't like her," he said quietly. "You won't like Kathryn." Your mother? he thought. *I* brought you up.

There was a sourness in his throat. He knew Kathryn. All Terri had to do was get in touch with her —that would be it. These years he'd devoted to her— down the drain . . .

"Does Aunt Vivian have a phone?"

"Yes."

"In her house?"

He hesitated. Habit of years. Then, "Yes," he said.

"You told me, you both said—she had to call from a booth—"

"Well, it was necessary . . ." He felt weary. So many questions . . . all the little strategies being brought out, exposed, scrutinized. He rubbed the back of his neck.

"What is it? What's Aunt Vivian's phone number?"

"I don't think I'm going to give it to you."

"Why?"

Barkley put his paws on the table and licked ice cream dripping down the side of the container. "Down, Barkley!" The dog had never been trained right. Terri spoiled him. Maybe his fault—he had a tendency to indulge her. Not that she was *spoiled,* but not used to his flatly refusing something she wanted. He saw on her face, in the sharpening of her bones, how much she wanted Vivian's phone number.

He thought of Vivian's defending him, explaining everything to Terri. *Yes, perhaps your father acted hastily, but always out of love, Terri. Remember that!* Hadn't she said exactly that to *him,* when he first took

113

Terri? After a month he'd gotten in touch with Vivian. Over the phone she had scolded, cried, and finally defended him to himself. *I know you did it out of love, Philly.* She had wanted him to come back, to give up Terri. He'd told her, No, no, *no*. And she knew that if she wanted to hear from him again, she had to go along . . .

"I only want to talk to my mother," Terri said. "You don't know where she is. Maybe Aunt Vivian does."

Her eyes were huge. He felt a weakening, wanted to touch her glossy, sweet-smelling hair, give her what she wanted. "Terri—" How to explain? "I can't help you. It would be cutting my own throat. I can't do that." He was fighting for her again. He had to do anything he could.

In bed that night Terri thought she heard every sound in the house—the refrigerator buzzing, her clock ticking, the linoleum creaking on the floor, even the secret, silent humming of electricity. If only she could be that silent, invisible, and full of power, she would find her mother, and go and look at her, see who she was and what kind of person. She felt a tugging, something unseen and powerful pulling her toward her mother. She got out of bed and wrote WHY WON'T YOU HELP ME? in red crayon on white paper. She did this six or eight times and then quietly went around the apartment taping the signs on the TV and the bathroom mirror and his bedroom door. WHY WON'T YOU HELP ME?

In the morning she didn't hear the alarm. When she got up, her father was gone and all the signs had been taken down. That day, she stopped speaking to him. She had never done anything like this, and it took all her courage. The silence went on and on. "This isn't like you," her father said. She didn't answer. Her hardness shook her.

"When are you going to talk?" he said.

That one time she answered. "When you tell me Aunt Vivian's phone number."

Monday afternoon in school there was a fire alarm during gym. "Walk slowly and quickly to the nearest exit," the gym teacher shouted, pushing people together. Terri and Shaundra found themselves paired off.

Outside, Mr. Perluzzi, the vice-principal, yelled through a megaphone, like a football coach. "Come on, let's get out here! Move it! Move it!" Kids and teachers milled around. A thick column of black smoke erupted from the chimney. Everyone seemed to see it at the same time. "Teachers, is everyone out of the building? Quiet, please. QUIET," he bellowed. "We're having a little trouble with the boiler. Nothing serious, but because of potential trouble, school is dismissed for the rest—"

Cheers, whistles, and screams of approval drowned him out. There was a stampede into the building for books and clothes. Shaundra and Terri were swept along and walked to the locker room together. "Well, see you," Terri said.

"Yeah, see you."

Neither of them moved. "Do you want to make up?" Shaundra said coolly.

"Do you?"

"I don't mind."

"I don't, either." Terri matched Shaundra's coolness.

"You don't sound very enthusiastic."

"Neither do you." Suddenly, wanting something clean and truthful, she said, "I do want to make up. I missed you. I missed you a lot."

The effect of her words on Shaundra was amazing. Her whole face changed, softened. "I've missed you, too, Terri," she said.

They got dressed and went to Shaundra's house. In Shaundra's room, with the door closed, and both of them sitting on the bed, Terri told Shaundra about her father and mother.

Shaundra pushed her hair behind her ears. "Terri? That really happened?" Terri nodded. "How can you be so calm? I'd be screaming and running around. *Kidnapped*. And your mom really *alive*. You're like a lake, Terri, a calm lake, and you're just *unruffled*."

"Calm?" she said. "Me?" She looked down at her hands pleating the bottom of her sweater. She started to laugh and found herself crying. Shaundra put her arms around Terri. "There, there," she said. "There, there." And for some reason it was immeasurably comforting to Terri to be patted on the back and hear Shaundra croon, "There, there . . . there, there . . ."

When Terri got home she found a note from her father on the refrigerator saying he'd gone out to pick up Chinese food for supper, and Barkley was with him. She went into her room. She was troubled . . . her father . . . her silence . . . When would she speak to him again? Nothing had changed. But how long could she go on this way? She sprawled on her bed, and only then saw the envelope on her pillow. It was a plain white envelope addressed to Vivian Mueller Eyes, 3547 Oakhurst Drive, Los Angeles, California 90313.

Fifteen

"Daddy," Terri said, "thank you for Aunt Vivian's address."

After a moment he said, "Okay." He dug into the spinach casserole in its ruffled aluminum tin. "You having some of this?"

"No, it's for you." She didn't like spinach, had put the frozen casserole in the oven to please him. "Eyes—what a funny name," she said, trying to draw him into a conversation. "Is that Aunt Vivian's husband?"

"Yes. That's Ray. Raymond Eyes."

"When did she get married?"

"Viv? Years ago. Way before I did."

"Does she live—are they poor?"

"Not particularly," he said. "Ray has a good job. He's a toolmaker, and Viv manages the shoe store now."

She ate slowly, understanding again, and again, each time with a fresh little shock, that *nothing* was as she had thought, as she had been told. Led to believe.

She looked up to see her father watching her. "Well —so, what now, Terri?"

She had thought about this, of course. "I'll write Aunt Vivian and ask her where my mother is."

He pushed back his chair. He felt tired. He had tried to hang on, but Terri had defeated him with simple silence. Her silence had told him that, bit by bit, he was losing her.

"Daddy—" Terri said. She came around the table, sat in his lap, and put her arms around his neck. "But you shouldn't . . ." he said. He felt the wetness in his eyes. "You shouldn't do this, you're getting too old for this."

"Oh, be quiet," she said, hugging him. "Be quiet, you big bozo."

"Hello?"

"Shaundra—hi, it's Terri."

"Hi, Terri! I didn't see you after school."

"I was making up a quiz."

"So what're you doing now?"

"I—what're you doing, Shaundra?"

"I was reading. I love to read on a rainy day. You sound funny. Your voice is funny. Are you crying?"

"Not exactly."

"What's the matter, Terri? Did something happen? Terri? Say something, will you? Is it *bad?*"

"Shaundra, it's good and bad both. I just got home and got the mail. I got the letter."

"The letter? You got it? From your Aunt *Vivian?* The answer from your Aunt Vivian? Did she tell you about your mother?"

"Yes . . ."

"She *knows* where your mother *is?*"

"Yes . . ."

"Terri. Oh, Terri, wow. I think *I'm* going to cry."

"Shaundra—it's not that good—it's—it's—"

"Terri, what's the matter? You *are* crying!"

"Shaundra, I have to hang up now, I'll talk to you in school tomorrow—"

"Terri, *wait*—"

"No, Shaundra."

"Can't you just tell me what—"

"Shaundra, I'm sorry—I can't . . . I can't . . . I don't want to talk about it now."

"Terri? Terri?"

My dearest Terri,

I, too, do not know where to start my
letter. There is so much to say. I
can't even begin to tell you how I
felt when I saw a letter from you in
my mail. Disbelieving, overjoyed,
and frightened all at once!

My first feeling was, Thank god
Phil has finally unburdened himself!
Thank god he has finally told Terri
the truth! It's what I have wanted.
From the very beginning, I didn't
agree with what my brother did.
Never! Not for one moment. Yet,
ever since I have received your
letter I have been so upset that I
have put off answering you.

I can hardly understand myself. To
think of all the times I begged Phil
to tell you! And now that he has, I'm
afraid. I am afraid. This is like
Pandora's box. It's because of me
that the box has been opened, and now
there are fearful things in the air.

If only I had left things alone,
you wouldn't have heard us talking
that night. But, still, you were
asking questions before that, weren't
you? Maybe Phil could have gone on
a little longer, but I have the
feeling that you would have found out
the whole story some way or other.
So while part of me is scared,
another part of me is glad this whole
sad, sorry business is coming to
some kind of end. You know what your
father did, dear, and now we all just
have to go on from here.

If I'm not being completely clear,

bear with me. There are so many
things I want to tell you. For
instance--yes, of course, the picture
of the boys in my wallet is important.
They are my sons, your cousins,
Jimmy and Dave, and oh, how much I
want to see all of you together
again!

But let me answer the question I
know must be most on your mind. Yes,
I do know where your mother lives.
She's kept in touch with me through
the years, always with the hope that
I'd have some news about you. I
wonder if you can understand how I
felt every time she called and I had
to deny what I knew was true? The
hardest thing I've ever had to do
in my life has been to tell her that
I had heard nothing, knew nothing.
(And besides this, every year when I
came to visit you and Phil, I've had
to make my husband and sons believe
I was just going away for a few days,
a little vacation on my own.) No,
they never knew. No one knew. I
promised Phil I wouldn't tell and
I kept that promise, even though
many times I felt it was too much to
keep to myself.

Even now I haven't told anyone,
not even Raymond, my husband.

I always knew if I broke my promise
to Phil I wouldn't see either of you
ever again. But if only I could have
told Kathryn, just once, what I knew
about you! So many nights I lay
awake and thought how much I wanted
to tell her, "Your daughter is

growing up a lovely, fine, sweet, and smart girl who would make you proud." We're both mothers. I _knew_ how she felt.

Well, so, now you are thinking, Terri, that the cat is out of the bag and why doesn't your talkative old aunt get to the point and tell you where your mother is? And tell her where _you_ are?

Terri, darling—if only it were that simple. _If only—_

But you see, Terri, if Kathryn knows where you are, your father is in danger. He committed a crime when he took you from your mother. And to tell you the truth, I do not know what she would do if she knew where he was. She could have him arrested. I love my brother. How can I do anything that might help put him in jail?

But how can I keep the truth from you? At this point, especially! Enough has been taken away from you. You said in your letter to me that you were old enough to know. I pray so! Because you will have to be the one to choose.

Maybe just knowing your mother is alive is enough for you. Can you be satisfied with that? When you're older, you could make the decision to go to your mother. Otherwise, you have to face the possibility that your actions could endanger your father.

It's up to you, Terri, darling.

I wish I could help you in your
decision. Sometimes things happen
that force people to grow up fast.
Terri, darling, think hard before
you do anything.

                    Much love,
                    Aunt Vivian

Kathryn Newhouse
525 N. Bassett Avenue
Oakland, California 99528
415-382-0591

"You were in my dreams last night," Terri said to
Shaundra as they stood in the lunch line.

"I was? That's great. Uch, look at those veggies.
They look malnourished. What was I doing in your
dreams?"

"Giving me advice."

"Was it good?"

"I don't know. I wish it was true." Shaundra smiled,
but Terri meant it seriously. "You said, 'You can, *too*.
I have the solution.'"

They sat down with their trays. "That doesn't sound
like much advice to me," Shaundra said. Terri took
her aunt's letter out of her pocket and spread it in
front of Shaundra. "Oh," Shaundra said as she read.
"Oh . . . Oh, no . . ." She turned the last page. "What
are you going to *do?*"

She shook her head. Now she had everything she
needed to find her mother—a name, an address, a
phone number—everything except the will to put her
father in danger. Was this what reporters meant when
they said, "Ironically enough"? "Ironically enough,"
just when she had all the information she had so passionately wanted, she couldn't use it.

End of the road. STOP. Go no farther. If You Pass
GO, Proceed At Once to Jail.

"I'm not doing anything." She sipped milk, could

hardly swallow. "I'm not going to get my father in trouble." She was aware of other kids sitting nearby and kept her voice low.

"It's not fair," Shaundra said. "I *hate* adults sometimes. I hate that they make us choose."

Terri pushed away her lunch tray. No appetite. None. "I don't know why I started all this," she said. She tried to laugh. "Oh, boy, am I feeling sorry for myself."

That evening, after supper, her father called Nancy. "I'd like to come over," he said. "Talk things over." His voice was almost musical. Terri, playing on the living room floor with Barkley, listened. "Yes," her father said. "I understand . . . All right . . . right . . . Yes . . . I'll see you in half an hour then. I love you— what? . . . But I *do* . . . All right, yes, for *now,* I agree I won't . . ."

A gust of wind shook the front window. Was Nancy changing her mind about her father? Did she understand now what he'd done? Did she think it was all right? Terri put her arms around Barkley nuzzling his clotted neck fur.

Her father came in, knotting a red plaid tie. "I'm going over to see Nancy." He smiled, sounded jubilant. "Is it raining out again?" He put on a jacket, ran his hands through his hair. "Will you be all right, honey? You don't mind, do you? You could come, but we have things to talk over."

"No, that's all right. You look nice."

He kissed the top of her head. For a brief moment she felt as if things were as they had always been— comfortable and loving.

He still wasn't home later after she showered. She left on the living room lights and went to bed. As many times as she had been alone in her life, she had never quite gotten used to it, but with Barkley sleeping on the floor next to her bed, it was all right. Again the wind came up and rattled the panes. She dug deeper under the covers and was half-asleep when the phone rang in the kitchen. She stumbled out of bed.

"Terri?" Shaundra said. "I know what you can do."

"Do about what? Shaundra, I was sleeping."

"Never mind that, Terri. Listen. What you do is, you call your mother, you tell her who you are, and then you say, 'You have to promise that you won't get my father in trouble. Otherwise, I can't keep talking to you.' If she doesn't promise right away, you just hang up so she can't have the call traced or anything like that. And if she *does* promise, you can talk to her."

Terri leaned against the wall. "Shaundra, do you really think it would work?" She stood on one foot, pushed the other cold foot against her leg.

"I don't know, Terri. I don't know your mother, maybe she just hates him so much—"

Terri made a choking sound. Barkley ambled into the kitchen, looking at her sleepily.

"The thing is," Shaundra said, "I figure—what else can you do? It's worth a try, anyway. Isn't it? Isn't it worth a try, Terri?"

Sixteen

"Hello?" a funny squeaky voice yelled.

"Hello," Terri said, "could I, ah—"

"Hello! Hello!" the squeaky voice screamed happily.

"—speak, could I speak to Mrs. N—"

"Hello! Hello! Good-by."

"Is Mrs. Newhouse there?" Terri looked at Shaundra, who was squeezed into the phone booth with her. Shaundra's bike was outside. They were holding hands. Shaundra's hand was hot, Terri's, icy. "Did I dial the right number?" she asked Shaundra.

"Yeah, you did. I watched you. What's the matter?"

"Hello! Hello! Answer the phone!" Squeaky voice screamed.

"It's a little kid," Terri said. What was she doing in a cold, dingy phone booth listening to a child halfway across the country scream in her ear? Who *was* this Mrs. Newhouse? Her mother? Who was *she?* A sour nausea climbed into her throat and she started to hang up.

"Don't," Shaundra said, pushing her arm. Then a man's voice came tinnily from the phone. "No, Leah, stop now—let Daddy talk—hello? hello?"

"Hello," Terri said feebly.

"Hello, I can't hear you."

She cleared her throat and brought out, "I'm calling for Mrs. Newhouse."

125

"She's not in right now. I'll take a message."

"Uh, um, when will she be in?"

"I don't expect her until about nine tonight."

"Oh. How about tomorrow? About this time?"

"She should be in then." He sounded impatient. "Who should I tell her called?"

"Terri."

"Who?"

"Terri."

"Your last name?"

"I'll call again," she said quickly. "Thank you, good-by—"

"Hold it, please," he ordered. "Is that Terri with a y or an i?"

The way he repeated her name frightened her. Had she been on the phone long enough for him to have the call traced?

"You want to talk to Mrs. Newhouse? Do you mind if I ask you what about?"

"Well, it's— I just want to talk to her. I'll call again." She hung up. "Let's get out of here," she said, pushing Shaundra.

"You didn't talk more than three minutes. What's the rush?"

"I think he knew who I was." She was sweating, could smell herself. "He wanted to know my last name. What if he was having the call traced?"

"Don't be paranoiac. How could he get in touch with the phone company when he was talking to you?" That was reasonable, but Shaundra sounded uneasy, too.

Terri opened the booth door and a gust of cool, wet air blew in. A police car slowly turned the corner. She remembered Aunt Vivian's question. Is knowing the truth enough for you? Why hadn't she been able to say *Yes* to that, and be satisfied? The phone rang. "You answer," she said to Shaundra.

"Hello? Yes, operator . . . Okay . . . right . . ." Shaundra covered the receiver and rolled her eyes.

126

"Woo, woo, what a voice! He says you owe money, Terri."

She put dimes and quarters into the slots, her eyes fixed on the blue and white cruiser slowly drifting down the street toward them.

"One more quarter," Shaundra directed. "Okay, operator? Thank you! You have a nice day, too."

"Hang up," Terri said. The police cruiser passed. They walked in the opposite direction, Shaundra pushing her bike.

On Denver Street a woman wearing a long brown coat and running sneakers came up to them and said in a rapid, urgent voice, "Girls! I heard that General Motors is going bankrupt tonight. Don't worry, the Canadians have more Chevys than we do." She put her hands on the handlebars of Shaundra's bike. "You've got the right idea. Drive a bike." Under her coat she wore several layers of sweaters. She had a small, peaked face and cropped hair. "A car drove into my bedroom last night. They were out for me, drove right over my bed. I'm thinking of going to Pennsylvania. Pennsylvania has immunity."

"Gee, that's great," Shaundra said. "Well, we gotta go now." She pushed her bike firmly past the woman. "One of your friends?" she said to Terri.

Terri looked back at the woman. What if her mother was a person like that? It was possible; anything was possible. She could be mental, a cold fish, a nasty, sneering, unpleasant person. After all, her father was warm, affectionate—whatever he had done, it had been out of love. Why hadn't he and her mother stayed together? It must have been her mother's fault. He had hinted as much. Should she really call again tomorrow?

At her house she didn't want to go inside. What if Mr. Newhouse had called the phone company the moment she hung up? *Trace that call.* Computers could do miracles. Maybe right now the police were in the neighborhood making a house to house search for someone named Terri.

"Let's go have something to eat. A hamburger."

"I don't have any money," Shaundra said.

"I do."

"No, you spent money on me the other day."

"I didn't. When was that?"

"In Shorty's. Remember—the hot fudge sundaes?"

"It doesn't matter. I'll buy—"

"No, I can't pay you back, Terri."

"I don't care."

"Well, I do. If you want a hamburger, I'll go with you. But I'll have a glass of water."

"You're stubborn sometimes, Shaundra!"

"Well, tough turkeys, Terri!"

They were on the verge of fighting again. Terri knew it was her fault. There was a knot in her belly. She took a deep breath. "Okay, let's go upstairs. Want to help me deflea Barkley?"

"Does it cost anything?"

"I'll let you help for free."

"Do I get a glass of water, too?"

"And a piece of apple pie." They went inside. "I'm sorry," she said, "I'm just nervous about the phone call."

"That's okay," Shaundra said.

In the apartment, Terri got a towel and a can of flea powder, and while Shaundra held Barkley on the towel she rubbed powder into his fur. "He hates this."

"Who blames him? Would you like to have sick-smelling flea powder rubbed into your fur?"

"Don't hold him too hard."

"Don't worry, I'm not mistreating beloved Barkley."

Terri felt better, calmer, but in the back of her mind, all the time they were defleaing Barkley and later playing Monopoly, she half expected a loud knock on the door. *Open up! Police!*

It was dark when her father came home. "Hello, Mr. Mueller!" Shaundra gave him a big smile, full watt-age. And when they walked downstairs, she said to

Terri, "Well, anyway, if you had to be kidnapped, you couldn't have picked a nicer-looking guy to do it. Are you going to tell him about your phone call?"

Terri shook her head. "No, Shaundra. There's nothing to tell."

Seventeen

"There's George," Saundra said, lilting her voice as they sat down in the cafeteria. "Should I call him over?"

"Woof, woof, Shaundra."

"I didn't say he was a dog!"

Terri remembered seeing Shaundra and George that morning in the art room, their heads together. "I think he likes you, Shaundra. Do you like him?"

"Well, now that I know him . . . but we're just friends. It's you he likes."

"He never even talks to me."

"He *told* me he likes you. Remember when we were having our fight? He told me then."

"How come he said it?"

"Well . . . I was mad at you, so I brought up the subject. I admit I was hoping he'd say something nasty. But all he said were nice things."

"Like what?" Terri said, starting to smile.

"Oh, that you were pretty and really smart."

"You never told me."

"I forgot." Shaundra unwrapped a cupcake.

"Something important like that."

"Control yourself. I'm telling you now. *George likes you.*"

"Don't talk so loud!"

"Ye gads, you are touchy these days."

"I'm *sorry—*"

"And you're always saying you're *sorry*."

"Well, I am." Terri bit her lip. She *was* edgy. It was the phone call. It was everything that was happening to her, and everything that wasn't happening to her. It was being nervous about the danger to her father, and it was not knowing how things were going to work out.

Later, in the phone booth, she noticed she was calling at almost exactly the same time as the day before. For once she was glad Shaundra wasn't with her. She really loved Shaundra, but she was too nervous to want her there.

On the first ring, a woman answered. "Yes! Hello?"

"Is this—may I speak to Mrs. Newhouse, please?"

"Speaking."

"This is Mrs. Newhouse?"

"Yes. Who is this?"

Terri wet her lips. Cars passed on the street. Whisk! Whisk! Whisk! It had snowed a little that morning, then melted. The streets were wet.

"Hello," the woman said. "Hello! Is this the person who called me yesterday?"

"Yes," Terri got out. Her heart thumped erratically. She had forgotten everything she planned to say.

"Who is this? Please—" Her tone was sharp. "If you have something to say, say it. What is this about? Who are you? I don't like bad jokes!"

"This is—it's Terri," she said in a low voice.

"Terri? I can't hear you. Where are you calling from?"

"I'm not going to tell you that."

"What did you say?"

She took in a lungful of air. "This is Terri. Are you my—is this Kathryn Mueller?"

"Did you say Terri? How do you spell that?"

Nothing was happening the way she'd imagined. "T-e-r-r-i."

"Terri who?"

"Terri Mueller. Mueller with an *e*."

131

"Who told you to say that? Is this a trick? Is this some kind of stunt?"

She was dizzy. She must have been hyperventilating, breathing too fast and taking in too much oxygen. The glass phone booth rushed around her.

"I *said,* Is this a stunt? How did you get that name? You know what I think of you people? People like you! I think you are sick. Sickos!"

"I'm Terri Mueller," she said, numbly.

A moment later the man she had spoken to the day before was on the line. *"Who is this?"* His voice was rough.

"Terri Mueller." The phone booth had slowed down, but now her feet burned as if the floor was on fire.

"Where are you calling from? What do you want?"

"I want to talk to my m—to Kathryn Newhouse."

"Why do you want to talk to her?"

"I want to know if she's my mother," Terri whispered.

"Look," he said. "Whoever you are—" Now he spoke slowly, emphatically. "I am not going to have her put through hell again for the sake of some stupid stunt. Do you understand?"

She shook her head. She didn't understand anything. "I'm Terri," she said. She couldn't think of anything else to say. "I'm Terri. Terri Mueller. If you don't believe me, call my aunt, my Aunt Vivian—"

"Who?"

"Vivian Mueller—no, Vivian *Eyes,*" she said, thinking that now he would never believe her. Why hadn't Vivian married a man named Jones?

"Who is she?" he said. "Where'd you get that name?"

"She's my aunt." She began to feel as disconnected from reality as the woman on the street who had told them a car drove over her bed and Pennsylvania had immunity. "She lives in Los Angeles. You can call her, and she'll tell you who I am." Who am I? she wondered as soon as she said it.

"Wait—wait—" His voice had changed. "Terri—Terri, are you there?"

"Yes."

"Would you mind answering a few questions? How old are you?"

"Thirteen."

"When's your birthday?"

"April."

"April what?"

"April eight."

"What's your father's middle name?"

"James."

"What's your middle name?"

"Lee. Terri Lee Mueller."

"Okay, okay, hold on. Hold it a moment. Kathryn," he yelled. "Come here. Talk to her. I think it's her."

"Terri?" the woman said. "Is this really Terri? *My* Terri? My Terri?" she repeated.

"Are you—are you my—are you Kathryn?"

"Yes. And you're Terri?"

"Yes. I'm your, I'm your—" She couldn't go on.

"Terri," her mother said. She was crying.

Tears came to Terri's eyes. She stood in the phone booth, listening to her mother crying in California, and crying herself.

"Terri, is that really you?"

"Yes, it's me. Why didn't you believe it was me?"

"This has happened before," she said. "Someone calling, saying, This is your long lost daughter, and then—Oh! Such cruel people! People can be so cruel." She was crying again. "This time it's true, though? It's you?"

"It's me," Terri said, her voice thick.

"Where are you? Are you with Phil? You've come back, is that it? He's brought you back? I want to see you! When can I see you? Are you here in Oakland?"

"I'm—I'm far away," Terri said. "I'm calling long distance."

"But you're in California?"

"No, no. I'm far away." And then in a rush, "I can't tell you where I am."

"Why not? Why can't you tell me? Terri, I've got to know. I want to see you. My god, please, where are you?"

"I can't let my father be hurt," she said softly.

"What? I don't understand."

"You could—what he did—I won't do anything to hurt him. You have to—" She faltered, couldn't say, *You have to promise me* . . . She didn't know how to talk to her, this woman who was her mother. She heard her mother's voice, heard her crying, but she didn't know who she was, or what she was thinking, or how much she hated Terri's father.

"If I told you about him," she said, "you could have him arrested." Her face burned. What if her mother hadn't known that? Why had she said it?

"Does Vivian know where you are?" Her mother was onto something else.

"Aunt Vivian won't tell," Terri said.

"She knows?" She answered herself. "Of course she does. That's why you said to call her. *She knows!* I always thought so." Suddenly she almost screamed. A long hoarse cry of pain. "She knows. She always knew!" Behind her, Terri heard the sounds of a child's voice. After a moment, her mother said, "When can I see you?"

"I don't know. I can't get Daddy in trouble. I won't—"

"Trouble? He's already in trouble!"

Alarmed, Terri said, "I better hang up now."

"No, no, no. *Wait.* Please. All right, I understand. You're protecting Phil. Is that right? That's it, isn't it? Oh, my dear," she said, "I hate that man. For god's sake, *I hate that man,* but he is as safe with me as he would be with his poor mother. God rest her soul," she added. "I want to *see* you. All I want is to see you again."

"Do you—do you pr—"

"I *promise* you," her mother said. "Do you think I'd do anything now, *the least thing,* that would keep me from seeing you? I promise you in every way I can think of to promise, that if you will come back to me, I won't do anything to Phil."

"Should I visit you?" Terri said.

"Visit? I want more than that! After all these years —*yes,* I want more. And you, Terri, you—what do you want?"

"I—I don't know," she said.

For a moment there was silence, then her mother said, "Oh, my dear, I'm sorry. I don't mean to press you. How do you want to do things? *Will* you come to visit? Please come. Please come right away."

"Well, there's school," Terri said. "And—I don't know what Daddy will say—"

"Yes, Daddy. Must consider Daddy. *Daddy,*" she said. "Oh, that liar! He's the only man I have ever—" She stopped. Terri heard her draw in breath. "I'm sorry. I didn't mean to say that. It's wrong of me. Sorry," she said again in a softer voice. "I'll try not to do that again. Let's just talk calmly. You're thirteen. A young woman. You were a baby the last time I saw you." Terri thought her mother was going to cry again. "Eight years," she said. "Eight years . . . eight years . . ."

"I have to hang up now," Terri whispered, near tears.

"No, don't, not yet. Let me call you. Tell me the number there—"

"I can't."

"Terri, I promise you—!"

"I'll call you," Terri said. "I'll call you again."

"Oh, please," her mother said. "When will you call me? Terri, don't let me lose you now that I've just started to find you."

"I'll call again," Terri said. "I promise."

135

"And do *you* keep your promises, Terri?"

She wanted to say her father had brought her up to be honorable. "Yes," she said. "I do." And for the first time she realized that her mother didn't know *her*, either. They were truly strangers to each other.

Eighteen

"Shaundra? Hi, were you in bed already?"

"No, that's okay. I was watching TV. Why are you whispering?"

"Can you hear me okay? My father's in the living room. I just wanted to talk to you privately. Listen, I told him. I told him I called my mother. I started to tell him that she cried, but he said, *'Don't,* Terri. Not unless you want to lay a lot of guilt on me.' So I didn't say anything else."

"Gee, *tough!* Did that make you feel real bad?"

"Shaundra, I *wish*—I wish I could just see her, and not have to tell him, or talk to him about it. It would be so much better if I could just do it, and not make *him* feel bad."

"Well, you can't, Terri. I know what you mean, but you can't. You never *can* do things that way. They won't let you."

"Hello," Terri's mother said.

"Hello, ah—ah—. Hello, this is your—this is Terri."

"Terri! Hello, Terri! How *are* you?"

"I'm good. I just came from school."

"Oh, this is wonderful that you called. Leah is taking a nap, and I was thinking about you."

"You were?"

"I was. I always think about you. Not a day has passed for eight years that I haven't thought about you."

137

"Oh! Who is Leah?"

Her mother paused. "Leah is your sister," she said. "Your little sister. Merle is her father."

Stupidly, Terri was shocked. Her *sister*. She had a sister? Yes, Leah, the telephone fiend, was her sister. And Mr. Merle Newhouse was her stepfather.

"Merle," she said, "—he's not the man you were going to marry?"

"Merle and I have been married four years."

"No, I mean the man who was going to teach in Italy, in the American School in Milano."

"How odd that you know that! How do you know that?"

"Daddy—"

"Phil remembered Clem?"

"Yes, he told me. Did you go to Italy with him?"

"No, of course not! Phil had stolen you, I couldn't—"

"Please don't say that! Please don't say he stole me." Her head began to ache. "He—took me."

"Ahh, I see. Well, to me, you were—I'll say, lost. Lost to me. You were *lost* to me." In a moment, she went on. "After that, leaving the country was out of the question. I didn't know how long you'd be—gone. I kept hoping, praying. He'll bring her back. Every day I woke up and thought, Today. He'll bring her back today. I couldn't go to Italy. I couldn't even go across the street, for months, for fear the phone would ring, and it would be Phil saying he was bringing you home."

Terri toed a greasy paper toward the door of the booth. The phone booth was like a little island, had even come to seem homelike in a grungy way. She didn't want to talk about her father. Today Kathryn said his name without emphasis, but Terri felt her mother's hostility slip through like . . . something raw.

"Terri, will you send me a picture? What do you look like?"

"I'm tall—"

"You are? I am, too."

"I know. Aunt Vivian told me."

"And what else? What color is your hair? It used to be the most beautiful silky black—"

"It's not silky, not really. It's dark and pretty long."

"You know what I wish? I wish I could just put my arms around you this instant. I dreamed about you last night. You were a little child and I was holding you, hugging you. Terri? When are you coming? *I want you here.*"

"I have to talk to Daddy."

"I know, I know, we need to take this thing in steps. Is that what you're thinking? And I'm impatient. I don't want to *wait* for anything."

Terri made some sound of agreement. Thinking? She didn't know what, or if anything, she was thinking. Cars slapped past spraying up water. She had wanted this—the right to talk to her mother, to know her. She hadn't thought any further. Now her mother wanted her to come *at once*, while her father didn't want to hear her mother's name. She saw that her hand on the phone was strained white. Why had she thought finding her mother would be one simple explosion of happiness? In fact there had not been a single moment she could pinpoint—*here . . . now . . . this instant . . .* when all feelings came together, when it was simply—*good.*

"I'm trying to form an opinion on you from your voice," her mother said. "I keep wondering if you're the same person you were when you were five years old."

"I don't know. I don't think so. What was I like then?"

"Like a rubber ball. Nothing could keep you down. Loved to skip and run. *Ran,* never walked anywhere."

"Do you remember a lot of things like that about me?"

"Not enough. After you were gone, I wanted to remember everything. It grieved me so that my memory was faulty. Terri, this call is going to cost a fortune. I can't let you keep spending money this way. I want to talk—I could talk to you all day. Give me your phone number and let me call you—"

"No, I can't. Not yet."

"Does Phil know you're talking to me?"

"I told him I called you."

"Well, then—? Is he anxious? I understand. All right? *I understand.* Look, ask him to call me, and *I* will reassure him that he's in no danger from me." Terri heard the deep intake of breath. "Let's all agree the past is the past. All I want now is to see my daughter and get to know her again. *I want you to come here.* Will you have him call me, Terri?"

"I'll talk to him," she said. She wanted to hang up and cry, and she didn't know why all this was so hard. "I'll call you back tomorrow."

"Terri? You can call me Mother. Or Mom. Or—"

"All right. Thank you."

"Thank you!"

Terri winced. She, too, had heard the primness of her words. Why couldn't she be spontaneous and warm? For a moment she hated herself, her mother, her father. . . .

"Look," her mother said, "*Kathryn* is okay. If that's what you want to call me, if that's how you feel comfortable."

"Thank you," Terri said again, more softly, meaning it.

"So—good-by for now, Terri. I love you."

She went into a photobooth in Wess's Variety Store, pulled the green curtain, and took five snapshots of herself. She didn't like them. In each one she appeared to stare beyond the camera into something unseen—a spacey look—and besides, her nose seemed angled, distorted. Her mother would think she was *ugly*. She tore up the pictures.

Nineteen

"What do you mean, you don't want to ask your father for the money for the airline ticket?" Shaundra whispered. They were in the neighborhood theater watching a movie about two teenage girls competing to see who could lose her virginity first.

"Shaundra, don't you understand anything?" Terri passed the box of popcorn and stared at the screen where one of the girls, wearing shorts and a tee shirt, was dousing herself in the shower to get the "wet look." "It was bad enough when I told him I wanted to go visit her."

Shaundra poked her. "What a dope!"

"Who, *me?* Or her?" Terri nodded at the girl on the screen.

"*Both* of you. Your father has the money, doesn't he?"

"Yes . . ." In the aisle across from her some kids were having a popcorn fight. On the screen, the girl in the wet tee shirt was trying to interest a boy who went to her school. *She* looked about twenty, and *he* looked about twenty-five. It was all sort of funny, but totally unreal.

"So ask him for the bucks," Shaundra said. She didn't take her eyes off the screen, or her hand out of the popcorn box. "How are you going to get out to California, otherwise? Your wings aren't fully formed yet."

"My aunt sent me some money. Did I tell you? And I have money saved up."

"How much more do you need?"

"*Lots.* Maybe I could get a job."

"Maybe you should ask your father."

"I'll think about it."

Shaundra turned and looked at her. "Oh, you lie. I can already see that stubborn expression on your face. Why is it so important to do it *yourself?*"

Behind them, someone thumped on Terri's seat. "Will you two dopes shut up!"

That was the end of the discussion until they came out of the movie. Terri blinked. The film had taken place in, of all places, California—lots of sun and blue ocean and wide expanses of beach. She pulled her hat down a little more snugly over her ears.

"What a gorpy movie," Shaundra said. "Will you tell me what's so awful about asking your father?" She broke off, poking Terri in the ribs. "Look who's coming! What's he doing here?" It was George Torrance. "Hiii, George," Shaundra said.

"Hi, Shaundra. Hi, uh, Terri." He flipped his long striped scarf over his shoulder.

"We just went to that movie," Shaundra said.

"Was it good?"

"Semi-good."

Terri and George stared at each other.

"You live around here, don't you?" he said.

"I told you she did," Shaundra said. "Ooops! Was I supposed to say that?"

George's forehead got red. Terri felt sorry for him, and something else, too—not nice, but true—bored. "Where do you live?" she said, giving him a special smile to make up for her mean thought.

"Brown Road. Over that way." He waved vaguely.

"Maybe we'll come visit you some day," Shaundra said. "*I* will, anyway, because Terri is going to sunny California."

"No kidding!"

"If I can get the money."

"She could get it from her father," Shaundra said, "but she's too stubborn."

"Shaundra, I just think it would be better if I did it myself."

"Okay, okay, mule. Do it your own way. Maybe you'll get out there in a couple more years."

George looked from one to the other of them, but his glance, Terri thought, lingered longest on Shaundra. They talked a few more minutes, then parted. "George is so cute," Shaundra said, with a sigh. "Don't you just wish you could wrap him up and take him to California with you?"

Terri laughed.

"No, I mean it. If *I* was going to California, I'd miss him," Shaundra said.

"Yeah, and six other boys, too."

"No, George most of all."

"Tell you what," Terri said. "If I do get to go out to California, I'll leave you my blue angora sweater—"

"You will!"

"—my Icelandic hat—" She pulled it more firmly down over her ears. "—and I'll leave you George Torrance, too," she finished.

"Terri!" Shaundra squeaked. Color filled her cheeks.

"And when I come back," Terri went on, "you can return my sweater and my hat."

"Terri? Hi, it's me, Shaundra. I can't talk long, I'm supposed to wash the dishes. I just wanted to tell you I have ten dollars for your California kitty."

"Now, look, Shaundra, just because I said I'd leave you George doesn't mean you have to—"

"Shut up, idiot. Ten dollars, okay?"

"I'm not taking your money, Shaundra."

"Yes, you are. Anyway, I'm not giving it to you. I'm lending it to you. There *is* a difference."

"Saundra, you have to work for—"

"Well, actually, I promoted a couple of loans off my

143

mother and Barry. Oh, wait—Here's Barry, he wants to tell you how wonderful he is."

"Hi, Terri! I wish I had some more money for you!"

"Barry, that's so *nice* of you."

"Uh, well, that's okay. Here's Shaundra."

"Terri? So you got ten more bucks, okay?"

"Shaundra, I—"

"No, no, don't tell me how fantastic I am. I know it, I know it. Bye, bye, Terri, see you Monday in school."

"Hi, Terri."

"Hi, Nancy! How are you? How's Leif?"

"Fine, honey, getting along fine. What I called for, do you think you and Phil would like to come to Thanksgiving dinner with me and Leif?"

"Sure! That would be wonderful."

"You want to check with Phil?"

"No, I know he'll want to. Nancy, do you know that I've talked to my mother? And that I might go out and see her?"

"That's exciting! I heard from Phil that you talked to her. I didn't know you had plans to visit, though. I'm so glad."

"Nancy? Was Daddy—did he feel really *bad* when he told you about me talking to my mother?"

"Let's put it this way, Terri. If it had been up to Phil, you wouldn't have known about your mother for another five years. If then. I know that for a fact. And I know for a fact that he still won't admit what he did was wrong. He's just stubborn and thick-headed on this point. I have talked myself blue in the face about this. He doesn't see what else he could have done, given the situation at that time. So, sure, he's upset now. You know how he feels about you. But he's pretty much facing reality. This *isn't* eight years ago. Things have changed, and he's got to swim with the tide. Of *course*, you called your mother. Of *course*, you're going to see her. And who knows what else? I keep putting myself in your mother's shoes, thinking if

I hadn't seen Leif in eight years and then he turned up—I don't know, I admire your mother's patience! I would have been in an airplane in a *moment,* flying out to you. So, when are you going to go?"

"I was thinking about Christmas vacation. I haven't asked Daddy yet."

"Terri, let me give you one word of advice. *Don't* let Phil give you a hard time—"

"He doesn't."

"—because you are totally within your rights."

"It's not that. It's just that the fare is really expensive."

"Well, Phil isn't on poverty row."

"I don't want to ask him," Terri said, bracing herself for the same arguments Shaundra had given her.

"I can understand that," Nancy said, surprisingly. "You have some money, don't you? What I think you should do is go full speed ahead. Make your reservations, start planning for the trip. Sometimes you've just got to have faith that things will work out. I'll tell you right now that I'm chipping in fifty dollars."

"Nancy, no, you can't—"

"What do you mean, I can't. Terri, *I* want you to see your mother. *I* want you to do this. If I had it, I'd give you the whole sum in a moment. Fifty dollars —that's just a token."

"I don't know what to say—thank you—"

"Don't say anything, Terri. I'm being selfish, doing this for *me,* as much as for you. Just go ahead and make the reservation; we'll get the money together, somehow."

Nancy set a festive Thanksgiving table. White cloth, sparkling crystal, and tall red candles burning at either end of the table, which was placed in the living room between the tall windows. She made a ten-pound turkey, candied sweet potatoes, stuffing, and vegetables. Phil and Terri brought pies, ice cream, and wine. It was too much food for the four of them. By the time

145

they finished sampling the second pie, Terri felt uncomfortably full. Leif, excited by the party atmosphere, had fallen asleep on the floor near Barkley.

"And now the dishes wait," Nancy said ruefully. She was wearing a long red hostess gown with silver embroidery around the stand-up collar.

"Don't speak of the dirty things." Phil took a small cigar from his breast pocket, nipped off the end, and lit it from a candle.

"I never saw you smoke."

"He doesn't," Terri said, "just on holidays."

"Well, it's very *sexy*." Nancy ruffled his hair. They were all laughing as she said, "I don't think your daughter's told you yet, Phil, but she's planning a trip to California."

Terri's stomach thumped. Right now she felt totally unprepared to discuss the visit to her mother. Her father looked startled, then wary.

"Well, did I speak too soon?" Nancy's face was flushed from the wine. "What do you say, Terri? Me and my big mouth . . . you know . . ."

"Daddy." Terri scraped bits of mince pie around on her plate. "My mother wants you to call her."

"Why?" He tapped ash on his dessert plate.

"She wants to tell you herself that you don't have to worry—you know, about her doing anything."

"Call her, Phil," Nancy said.

"Look, I don't have to do that."

"It would be a good idea. Call her, say hello, and get the details of Terri's trip settled."

"I just heard about this trip," he said.

"There's not that much time." Nancy glanced at Terri with a do-you-want-me-to-shut-my-mouth look. "She should go over Christmas vacation. Right? Don't you think so, Phil? So she doesn't miss school."

They looked at each other. Terri sensed a lot of unspoken things happening. Phil tap-tap-tapped his cigar on the edge of the plate and Nancy, fiddling with her wine glass, looked at him with a certain firm, challenging expression. "Phil, I want you to do this," she said.

"Don't push it, Nancy."

"You know what we talked about."

Terri felt their tension coiling inside her. She scraped back her chair. "Excuse me—"

In the bathroom she spit into the bowl, her stomach heaved, but she couldn't get anything else up. She rinsed her mouth, and combed her hair. Her color was high, almost feverish.

When she came back to the table her father said, "Do you know your mother's phone number?" Terri nodded. Her father wrote it down on a napkin and went into Nancy's bedroom. She and Nancy began clearing the table. She heard her father saying, "Kathryn? This is Phil." Then he closed the door.

A few minutes later, he came out, relit his cigar, and said, "You're going out on the nineteenth, Terri." He looked at Nancy, picked up a handful of dishes, and went into the kitchen. "I'll wash," he called. "You two dry and put away."

"Hello? Barry?"

"Yeah, this is Barry. That you, Terri?"

"Hi, Barry. Is Shaundra there?"

"The beast? Yeah, she's in her room."

"Will you get her for me?"

"Don't you want to talk to me? I'm much nicer than the beast."

"Give her a break, Barry."

"Awww, Terri, what for?"

"Barry, you going to call her or not?"

"Okay, okay, for you, Terri, I'll do it. Hey, BEAST, your friend is on the phone . . ."

"Hi, Terri!"

"Shaundra, guess what? My father talked to my mother yesterday."

"You're kidding! What'd they say?"

"I don't know. He didn't want to talk about it. Ex-

147

cept that he said I was going to California, and he gave my mother our phone number. After we came home from Nancy's she called and said she was sending me my ticket."

"*Fan*-tastic!"

"Yeah, only Daddy said, 'Nothing doing! This is on *me!*' And, Shaundra, then he called the airline and made the reservations."

"He did? He really did? You must feel fan*tas*tic."

"I don't know how I feel, Shaundra. I'm going. I'm going to California to see my mother. I keep telling myself that, but I don't believe it yet. I guess I just don't believe it, yet."

Twenty

Dear Daddy,

The plane trip is going okay so far. I'm sitting by the window, but I don't look out too often because it reminds me where I am--up in the air! They keep feeding us little tidbits--nuts in a silver paper package, and juices, and lunch, and more nuts and drinks. When we took off I must have turned green because, just by looking at me, my seatmate guessed it was my first flight.

She told me about her first airplane trip which she didn't take until she was 58 years old. She's 75 now! I wish you could see her. She's not even five feet tall and has the most beautiful white hair. She has 8 grandchildren and 5 <u>great</u> grandchildren. She's flown across the country seven times and <u>hates</u> to be called a senior citizen.

She took out her wallet and showed me her Grey Panther membership card. By that time we were in the air and she had really distracted me from being scared.

Well, I'll close now, Daddy.
They're going to show a movie. Take
care of yourself, I'll see you in
two weeks.

Love, Terri.

P.S. I just thought—this is the
first letter I've ever written you.
Also, the first time I've ever been
on an airplane. Also, the first time
away from you (in eight years).

P.S. again. Did you see what Nancy
gave me? It's a sort of diary, but
it says Journal on the front. It's
about half the size of a notebook
and has a beautiful leather-looking
cover.

P.P.S. Give Leif a big hug for me.

Dear Nancy,
  Here I am on the plane and writing
my second letter! (I just wrote to
Daddy.) I keep thinking of all the
firsts on this trip. My first time
in an airplane. My first time going
across the country in one day. My
first letter to Nancy.
  Last night I was thinking about
Daddy being alone for these two
weeks and how it will be our first
Christmas we haven't been together.
I didn't sleep too much. Excited
about the trip and sort of worried
about leaving Daddy. Then I
remembered that you and Leif will
be keeping him company, and that
made me feel much better.

I'm sitting next to this very nice
old lady who is really beautiful.
Her face is full of lines and
wrinkles, but I think that only
makes her more beautiful.

I keep thinking about my
grandparents who I'm going to meet.
My mother's mother and father. Did
I tell you their names? Ethel and
Robert.

Nancy, I love the journal. I was
really surprised when you gave it
to me. I hope I didn't sound too
dumb when I said, "What is it?"
And looking right at the cover where
it said JOURNAL! I thought it was
a book. When you said, "It's for
you to write in. You'll be glad
later on if you keep a record of
this trip," I finally realized it
was a diary. I kept a diary once
when I was ten years old. For one
week I wrote down everything that
happened to me. Then I stopped.
Anyway, I will try to keep this
journal. And I thank you for
thinking of me.

Love, Terri.

P.S. Isn't this nice writing paper?
Shaundra gave it to me.

Dear Shaundra,

I'm getting writer's cramp! I'm
not even in California yet, and
I've written letters to Nancy and
Daddy, and now you. I love this

writing paper! You and Nancy must
have had a secret conference. You
gave me writing paper, and she gave
me a journal.

They certainly do feed you on
these trips. I've been pigging it
up the whole time. So far I have
had four packages of salted roasted
peanuts, one glass of apple juice
(with ice cubes with holes in the
middle), one glass of tomato juice,
two glasses of ginger ale, one lunch
consisting of baked chicken, sweet
potato a la marshmallow, salad with
French dressing, milk, and
strawberry ice cream cake, AND one
crunchy chocolate nut bar given to
me by my seatmate!

Her name is René, she is wearing
a red pants suit, and red and white
striped blouse with a red bow in
her hair. Her glasses are blue,
have sparkles on the frame and a
tiny blue bird etched into the
bottom of one of the lenses. She is
reading a book about a movie star,
has a shopping basket filled with
goodies and is one of the
friendliest, peppiest people I have
ever met.

Now for the surprise. She's 75
years old! When I sat down next to
her she stuck out her hand, and
said, "How do you do, I'm René." I
said, "I'm Terri." She then said,
"This is my seventh trip across the
country." When we took off I guess
I turned a nice shade of green.

René said, "Have you flown before?"
I shook my head. She said, "Are
you worried?"

"A little," I said. Ashamed to
tell her my knees were knocking and
my hands were sweaty!

"Oh, it's as safe as being in a
bathtub," she said. "You know more
people get knocked off on highways
than ever do in airplanes." Then
she said, "Statistics don't lie.
And, anyway, if we do go down, it'll
be fast."

Comforting, eh?

Then she started telling me about
her life. She had to go to work
when she was 15 years old, never
finished school, but says she is
always learning. She told me about
her children and her grandchildren.
And her great grandchildren. It was
really interesting. And before I
knew it we were in the air and, as
they say, it's been smooth sailing
ever since!

Well, I'll sign off now. When
you put on your boots and down
jacket, think of me in sunny
California!

Love, Terri.

P.S. Did I ever tell you that the
last time I talked to my mother,
she told me my grandmother's name?
It's Ethel Moonchamps Susso. I
wonder if Ethel will be as pretty
and interesting as René. Anyway,
her name is interesting!

DEAR

HOW R U? 👁 AM FEELING 😊

HERE 👁 AM IN A HUGE ✈ TWA UP IN

THE SKY! 👁 AM SITTING NEXT 2 A VERY

NICE 🧑 WHO WEARS 👓 . HER 👀 R

BLUE LIKE THE SKY! ☁☀☁ MAYBE 🐝 U WILL

WRITE 🏃 A 🖼 WHEN 👁 AM IN

CALIFORNIA!

SEE U, DEAR 🍃 SOON!

XXXXXXXX,OOOOOOOOOO 👄

LOVE AND KISSES FROM, TERRI.

154

Twenty-one

On the plane. My seatmate, René, is snoozing, so this is a good time to write in this journal. It's funny I just wrote "snoozing." That's René's word. "Well, Terri, time for a little snooze." She got a pillow and a blanket from the steward and looks very comfortable. I should sleep, too. I'm pretty tired from not sleeping much last night, but every time I close my eyes, they snap open.

Last night, every time I woke up I would think about this trip—not about my mother, but what it would be like to go in an airplane. I don't especially like high places, and here I am looking out the window, and all I see are clouds below me. I am actually above the clouds. There must be things you know —with your mind—but somehow, you don't really know, not inside you. It's only now, looking down at those clouds, that the realness of space—the limitless-ness—comes to me. No, Terri, all that blue sky you see from the earth is not like the roof on a house!

I guess it's the same way I feel about going to see my mother. With my mind I know that's where I'm going, but inside me I still don't know it. Probably won't until I see her. Like seeing the clouds. Then— oh, yeah, it's really true!

Every time I get myself to actually think about it, my stomach jumps. I don't know what to expect. One thing Daddy said quite a while ago has been

155

bothering me. I don't remember when he said it, but I do remember what he said. "You won't like her." Whew! I didn't want to ask anything else. I just let it drop.

I'm scared. I haven't said it to anybody, not to Nancy, not to Shaundra, definitely not to Daddy. Part of the scared feeling has been that something would happen to keep me from going at all. But now I'm in the plane, and unless we crash, I'll be in Oakland in another hour. Now there's a comforting thought. If we crash, I won't have to worry about how scared I am about meeting my mother.

I'm really in a mood to write. All those letters, and now this journal. Maybe I will write in it every day. I'm writing down things I hardly even knew I was thinking.

Just took out the picture my mother sent me of herself. I left my sweaty fingerprints all over it. Gee, maybe my mother will take one sniff and send me back! If Nancy were here, I'd tell her that and get a laugh out of her. At the airport, she started telling jokes. "What's green and sour and bigger than a pickle jar?" "I don't know, Nancy." "A pickled elephant, Terri." We were both chortling, but I kept thinking she was going to cry.

All the people I especially love are really emotional. Even Leif is already that sort of person. This morning when we picked up him and Nancy he grabbed me around the legs and said, "Hello, Terri, my best Terri." Nancy says all kids are loving that way until something or somebody puts them down, out in the big bad world. Was I that way? I know that now I just don't freely give out my love and affection, I don't freely show it. I feel things, and I want to hug Nancy or kiss Shaundra. But then I don't. I press someone's hand and hope they know I'm feeling loving. I wish I could just grab and hug the way Nancy does.

Right now I'm remembering when Daddy and I said good-by. Sadness, a sad feeling. I got in the line to show my boarding pass. Then I turned around to wave good-by. Right then I should have run back and told him, "Daddy, I love you."

Why didn't I do it? Why don't I do things like that? Why don't I say the things I'm thinking and feeling? This is a serious fault of mine. I brood over things. Shaundra told me one time that I sit on my thoughts until they hatch. Right now I'm thinking, What if the plane crashes and I didn't say that to Daddy? Will he know? I tell myself, he knows. I wanted to write it in my letter, but I didn't. I just tried to make it very loving.

The NO SMOKING sign just went on. We're going to land in a few minutes. My stomach feels like a Mexican jumping bean.

Twenty-two

The airport was crowded. Terri carried her down vest over her arm, knapsack on her back, suitcase in her left hand. She stood near the gate, looking for her mother. Would she recognize her? A boy and a girl, both smiling eagerly, approached her. "Hello!" the girl said.

"Hello." Terri thought her mother had sent them to meet her.

"Isn't it a wonderful day?" The girl's smile had a special radiance, as if meeting Terri was the most fabulous thing that had ever happened to her.

"Is life being good to you?" The boy was very clean looking, his hair cropped short, his smile equally brilliant. Terri felt confused, smiled uneasily. Then the boy held out a book to her, on the cover a white-robed man with his hands raised. "Take the book, sister, it's a gift from Master Kufari."

At that, Terri realized they were cult people. "No . . . thank you." Half to get away from them and half because she was feeling a little frantic, she walked rapidly away, looking for her mother in the crowds of people. Despite the picture, she had no faith that she would know her mother when she saw her. As for her mother recognizing Terri—impossible. She had never sent a picture and had been five, only five, the last time Kathryn had seen her.

She stared at every woman. Her? . . . Her? . . . Her . . . ?

No . . . no . . . no . . . no . . . *no*. . . .

There was a soreness in her eyes. Where was her mother? They'd never find each other. Maybe she hadn't come, had changed her mind. Terri would wander around this airport all day, then go home, and that would be it.

She ran, dodging people, her suitcase bumping her leg. "Slow down there," a man said in a genial way. She didn't spare him a glance, kept running.

All at once she saw her. Saw her mother. She thought she saw her. A woman coming toward her, a tall woman with black hair loose around her face and deep-set dark eyes. The woman came closer, hurrying, looking straight ahead. *Her mother*.

Terri stopped. She saw her mother, she recognized her, and a feeling came over her as if everything had stopped. Everything was waiting . . . waiting . . .

Her mother . . . *Her mother*. There was an ache at the back of her throat, and she felt a fierceness of tears. And still she stared. Didn't speak. Couldn't speak. She felt something shimmering, something flowing and shaking through her . . . Her mother . . .

She was wearing almost the same clothes as in the snapshot she'd sent Terri. A light pleated skirt, a pink silky blouse, and strings of pink beads. A leather pocketbook with a long strap over her shoulder. A big, tense, elegant look to her . . .

There was a great amount of noise in the airport. People talking, planes taking off and landing, voices over loudspeakers demanding attention. "MR. AN-DREOLLI, report to American Airlines desk please." "MISS SUSANNE CHICKOUR, report to Trans World Desk at once." "I have a message for MR. ELLITON . . ."

Terri heard everything, and yet it was also as if all sound had been switched off. Everything was still, her mother in the center of the silence, and all the people silently streaming past Terri. Then her mother, too, passed her. It was like a dream. She stood there and watched her mother move out of sight, and couldn't move, couldn't call.

Someone bumped into her. "Oh, pardon." She hardly heard, but it seemed to jolt her awake. She walked after her mother, just walked, and then in a moment, she ran. She didn't feel anything now. She caught up with Kathryn and touched her arm.

Her mother turned and for minutes, it seemed to Terri, simply stared. Her eyes became huge and darker, her face got full of color. "Terri?" she said. "Terri?" Then, "Is it over? It's over, isn't it? It's over, it's really over."

They stood face to face. She took Terri's free hand. "Hello," she said. "You're so big." Her eyes got wet. She put her arms around Terri, and Terri, beginning to love her mother, felt something welling into her, something loosening.

Her mother raised her face. She was crying and said, "Don't cry, Terri. Don't cry. It's all right. It's all right now. It's done."

Terri didn't know she was crying. And then they held each other again, and she knew she cried, knew she was crying harder than she had ever cried in her life.

Twenty-three

"WELCOME HOME, TERRI!"

The sign, strung across the front of the small white stucco house, was the first thing Terri saw when her mother parked the car. "Merle's students made the sign," her mother said. "They did it as a surprise for him when they heard about you." The foot-high red letters painted on a white sheet were surrounded with yellow rays.

"They know about me?"

"Who doesn't?" Her mother stroked her arm. "After you called me that first time, I went on a real talking jag. Told everyone possible my daughter was coming home. You should have seen me, I even cornered poor old men in the supermarket and told them."

They got out of the car and walked up the stone path. Before they got to the door, it was flung open with cries of "Welcome!" "Surprise!" "Hello, Terri!"

"What is it?" she said.

"It's a party. Do you mind? I'm sorry, so many people wanted to see you. So many people were happy for us—I couldn't deny them—"

Her mother held Terri's arm tightly against her side, and they walked into a knot of smiling people who broke into applause. They moved from a small hall into a living room crowded with furniture. At the edge of the circle of people a young man held up a camera. A

161

flash bulb went off. Terri blinked. Hands reached out to her, grabbed, squeezed, patted.

"Terri, darling. Terri, darling! Oh, let me hug you." A husky woman with glasses, tears streaming down her face. "Sweetheart! My darling." Terri was stifled against her chest, smelled a musky scent, cigarettes, food. "Don't you know me? I'm your grandmother. I'm Gramma Ethel."

"My turn! My turn!" New arms took her. "I'm Bob, I'm Grandpa Bob." Those same brown speckled eyes as her mother, a full head of white hair, a stiff mustache that scratched her face. "So you're here, here at last." He squeezed her hands, his eyes were brimming, too. He wore jeans, and a pink cowboy shirt with pearl buttons.

"Gramma . . . Grandpa," she said awkwardly. Chills went through her, she shivered, her hands were icy. Flash bulbs exploded. She turned this way, that way. Introductions . . . neighbors . . . friends . . . "And this is Leah!" A thin face, suspicious brown eyes saying, Who is this intruder?

"Terri, I'm Merle." A tall, almost fat man with a dimple in his cheek, wearing plaid pants. "Can I kiss you, Terri?"

People . . . voices . . . smiles . . . Her hair tousled . . . arms and hands squeezed . . . Everyone beaming at her with good will. The curly-haired photographer from the newspaper stopped to say, "This must be a fantastic day for you."

"Yes," she said. "Oh, yes." Feeling dazed, hemmed in.

"Here's your sister, here's Terri." Her grandmother holding up Leah. "Come on, say hello to your sister!" At the command, scowling, Leah turned her head away.

"Eat, everyone, eat," Merle yelled. There was food, bottles of wine. "It's a happy day! Our daughter has come back!" Cheers, more applause.

Talk burst around Terri, little volleys of words.

"Isn't she beautiful? Looks just like Kathryn."

"No, I'm sure they said Wis*con*sin . . ."

". . . who *knows* what went on? I heard . . ."

Her grandfather took her aside. "I want to ask you something." He smoothed his mane of white hair with a careful hand. "Did your father treat you all right?"

"My father—of course."

"Yes?" he said, doubtfully. "Yes? He did?"

Then she understood his question covered other questions, bizarre, ugly thoughts about her father. *Who knows what went on?*

She stiffened. "Don't you know my father?"

"Oh, sure, I know Phil. Always thought well of him until—" He brushed his hair, brushed and brushed it. "Do you feel resentment toward him for what he did to you?"

"He didn't do anything to me." And who was this satisfied-looking white-haired man to say these things about *her father?*

Her grandfather's face fell; she thought he looked like Leif when he'd done something wrong. "Did I make you feel bad? I did, didn't I?" He squeezed her shoulder. "Well, look here, I'm sorry about that, I'm really sorry."

Her grandmother clapped her hands. "Quiet, everyone. It's time for the presents. Bob?" Her grandfather went into another room and returned with an armful of boxes wrapped in glittering paper. "Right here." Her grandmother indicated Terri, and the entire stack of boxes slid out of his arms in a heap at Terri's feet. There were oohs and aahs.

"Sweetheart," her grandmother said, "these are all the presents your grandpa and I bought for you every birthday and every Christmas for the past eight years." Applause. Tears in her grandmother's eyes.

Terri stared at the huge glittering mound. Her heart was beating very rapidly. "The past eight years." Did all these people hate her father? Her neck heated, she felt that soreness in her eyes.

163

"Darling, open them," her grandfather said. Behind her, Terri's mother smiled wistfully at her.

"Ethel has been waiting for this moment," her grandfather said. "She's going to enjoy this more than Terri."

Terri picked out a box, began to unwrap it.

"Don't worry about the paper," her grandmother said, "just tear it off." Terri continued to slowly unwrap the box. Ethel took it from her and ripped off the paper.

"You should let Terri do that," her husband said.

"Ooops!" A pink-nailed hand went to Ethel's mouth. "Am I being grabby?"

"Yes, Ma," Terri's mother said.

"Do you have to agree with me?" She adjusted her glasses. Everyone laughed.

"What's in the box? What's in it?" Leah asked. "Is it for me?"

"No, sweetheart, it's for Terri, it's for your sister, Terri," Ethel said. "She hasn't had presents in a *long* time."

"I have," Terri said. "I have!" She didn't realize how her voice clamored until a little silence fell.

Her grandmother held up a blouse with sprigs of flowers embroidered on collar and cuffs. "Isn't it beautiful?" She read the card that had been inside. "For my darling Terri on her ninth birthday." She handed Terri another box. "I promise not to touch this one!"

There were paints and drawing sets, dolls, dresses, socks, and little pocketbooks and brushes, books, records, and games. "Thank you," Terri said. "Thank you . . . thank you . . ." She felt the strained smile on her face. Opening the presents seemed to go on endlessly. She wanted to get away. "Thank you . . . Thank you, Grandma . . ."

At last it was over. She took a little checked cloth doll with a zipper down her back to Leah. "Look, you can put your pajamas inside." Leah took the doll. "I don't say thank you" she said, opening the zipper. Terri sat down next to the child. With Leah, at least, she felt

164

an uncomplicated emotion. Leah was jealous; Terri didn't blame her and hoped they could be friends. But all these other people she was suddenly related to—did she like them? Love them? Did they see *her?* Or Terri, the Long Lost Child?

She sat cross-legged, smiled automatically as people came up to touch her head, to say nice things. She hadn't thought how it would be. She had thought *Grandma . . . Grandpa . . . Mother . . .* And now they were Ethel, Bob, Kathryn . . . It was all strangeness. Was she happy at last? She couldn't tell. She felt numb, close to exhaustion.

That night, faces whirled in her dreams, and voices, color, movement. There was her grandmother, the bright red lipstick, the eager, grasping smile . . . Then her grandfather, with his soft, handsome, discontented, pouty lips, his mane of white hair . . . He brushed it, brushed it with his hand . . . and smiled with infinite satisfaction. "He has so much hair," her grandmother said in the dream. "Such thick hair, such a beautiful white color."

"Yes, but Merle already has a bald spot," Terri wanted to tell her, and she woke with that sentence in her head, thinking that they were all cartoons. All. Even little Leah, with her pointy, jealous face. Only her mother seemed real to her.

Twenty-four

On the morning of the first day her daughter Terri had
slept under her roof in eight years, Kathryn woke early.
At once she realized that for the first time in eight
years she had awakened without a dull band of pain
across the back of her head. She left Merle sleeping,
put on a robe, and went into the kitchen. From Leah's
room—the children's room, she corrected herself—
there was a sleeping silence. It was not yet six o'clock.

"Terri must be exhausted," she murmured to herself,
for the simple pleasure of her older daughter's name
so easily and possessively on her tongue. Moving quietly so as not to wake anyone in the slumbering house,
she fixed a cup of tea and took it to the window looking out over the backyard.

As she sat there, sipping the tea, she was again aware
of the *absence* of that clamp of pain. Even these past
four years when she had been happy again—Merle,
Leah—she had had to fight her way past that greyness
every morning. Past the shadow of the unanswered
questions about Terri. Where is she? How is she? Will
I ever see her again?

From the pocket of her robe she drew out the lami-
nated picture of Terri that she had slept with every
night under her pillow. And staring at the little Terri,
in pleated skirt and blouse, hands jauntily on her hips,
celebrating her first day of kindergarten, Kathryn
thought of this Terri she had now met. This tall sober

girl with the sudden beautiful smile, this girl-child with the intense dark eyes, this self-possessed almost-woman who looked, and listened, and looked, and said so little. This was not the child Kathryn had cherished in her heart all these years.

"*My* daughter—she's *my* daughter." She knew that her own reserve often bothered her mother. "Cry!" Ethel had demanded those first months after Phil and Terri disappeared. But Kathryn didn't cry. She faced the world dry-eyed, and inwardly raged. Raged and felt alone—cold and alone. She never could get her hands warm that first year.

She noticed a yellow bow on the floor, and a snip of silver paper, and picked them up. She smoothed the yellow ribbon. So many questions . . . the gap of years . . . the emptiness of those years . . . Could they ever be filled? Would she ever know her daughter the way other mothers knew theirs?

The lightness in her vanished. She reached for it . . . Oh, bring back that floating feeling! That joy to see the sun rise! Please! She thought of those first years. Working jobs where she could come in, be a robot, get out: typing, slinging hamburgers, selling movie tickets. All she did was work, and sleep, and badger Vivian with phone calls. She ran ads in newspapers up and down the coast of California. "REWARD for information about missing child . . ." Her guess had been that Phil wouldn't go far from what he knew. She'd been wrong about that.

Once she'd hired a detective—that had been worthless, and had cost her all her savings. A grey life . . . everything taken from her, the only reason to get up in the morning the hope that on this day Terri might be returned to her.

Twice in those years, newspapers had run feature stories about Kathryn. She had answered questions, allowed her picture to be taken. Everything private in her had protested, but she had submitted meekly in the hope that it might somehow, some way, help her find

Terri. And in the morning she had read the "heart rending" details of her life spread out in black and white to be served up to eager readers along with their coffee and toast. FATHER 'STEALS' DAUGHTER, MOTHER WAITS FOR HER RETURN. And next to the article a picture of herself in a white blouse, eyes sunk into her head, fondling a little scarf that had been Terri's.

But all that had come of it were the phone calls. *Hi, Mom, this is your long lost daughter . . . This is Terri, did you miss me?* And then the laughter.

She had wanted to move out of the apartment, away from the phone, away from the memories, but she was afraid. This was Terri's home. This was what she would remember. Terri knew her phone number. If she could get away and call . . . Night after night Kathryn sat home staring at the phone. Night after night she heard the child crying for her.

In the bedroom now she heard Leah chanting. A moment later, the sound of two voices. Her daughters. *Both my girls.* Talking together in her house. Dear god, it was over . . . it was over . . .

A few minutes later, hearing Terri in the shower, an anxious, bizarre thought occurred to her. How do I know that's really Terri?

She took another sip of tea.

The thought refused to go away.

What if Phil had played an elaborate hoax on her? What if, driven to the wall, he had sent another child in Terri's place?

Don't be stupid, Kathryn. Think of something else.

She put down her teacup. The phone conversation with Vivian a few days ago. "Don't be bitter," Vivian had said in that big husky voice of hers. "Kathryn, don't be bitter. I wanted this for you. I wanted this so much, you don't know."

"All right, Vivian," she had said. She had been quiet, controlled. Bitter? Vivian didn't know half her bitter-

168

ness, half her anger. Futile, futile! Useless emotions from another time . . . a time that was over. Done.

What if it isn't Terri?

She went to the bathroom, knocked. "Terri? Can I come in for a moment?"

The door opened; there was Terri, holding a towel around herself. "Hello," she said.

"Good morning." Kathryn felt a rush of tenderness for that young body, its lean strength, its newness. "Terri—could I see your shoulder?"

"What?" The dark eyes met hers.

"Your shoulder—your right shoulder." Gently she pulled away the towel, and there it was—that little odd-shaped birthmark she had kissed every night when she helped the child into her pajamas. "It's still there," she said, smiling, a little ashamed of her relief.

"My amoeba? Why did you want to see that?"

"Oh—" Kathryn spread out her hands. "I used to kiss it. I wanted to see it again."

Terri accepted this explanation as if, Kathryn thought, nothing adults did or said could any longer surprise her.

The first few days of Terri's visit, her mother hardly left her side. Merle did the shopping and cooking, kept Leah occupied and left her mother free to be with Terri.

That first morning, after breakfast, they went for a walk, a long walk that didn't end for hours, and they did this every day for several days: talking and walking.

They sat on a bench in a park and talked. After a while they walked again. Later in a playground, they sat on the swings, slowly drifting back and forth, and talked, then got up, talking still, and walked until, hungry, they went into a small restaurant, took a table in a corner near a window, and talked some more. When they left Terri didn't remember what they had eaten.

Talking and walking . . . and talking . . . and talking . . . Terri thought that never had she talked so long, so continuously, and with so much close attention paid to everything she said.

"I need to fill in," Kathryn said. "I need to know. All the years, all the months, weeks, hours . . . I want to know *everything*."

She asked question after question. "So, okay, you were seven years old then. Where did you say you were living? And that teacher, Mrs. Kane, was it?" And Terri drew on her memory of faces and places, of names and cities and apartments . . .

Kathryn leaned toward her. She wanted to know details. Who shopped for clothes for Terri? Were people kind to her? Had anyone ever been suspicious? What did Terri know or suspect about herself?

"Nothing, not really. Only . . . I felt something was wrong." More questions. What kind of food did they eat? Was Barkley her only pet? Did she like moving about all the time? What about school? How about when she was sick—who took care of her? Did she stay home alone?

"There was always someone around to look after me when I was little. Not now—I stay home alone."

"Were you ever really sick?"

"When I was eight, I think it was, I had measles."

"Who took care of you?"

"Daddy," Terri said in surprise. Who else?

"Phil? He took care of you? Didn't he have to work?"

Terri thought about it. Yes, she was sure her father had been with her through that entire siege. And the following winter when she'd had her tonsils out, he'd been with her through it all, operation and recuperation. "I guess he didn't go to work when I was sick." She had never given it a thought before.

The hardest thing Terri had to say was that her father had told her Kathryn was dead. But her mother laughed. "Killed me off in a car accident, did he? Phil comes on so gentle, oh, yes, I remember him. But he

170

has the same violent streak we all have." She seemed to draw a certain satisfaction from this.

On the fourth day of her visit the whole family went on a picnic. Her grandfather brought along a portable radio, tuned it to the San Francisco Opera Company. Merle, her grandmother, and Leah played ball, and Terri and her mother, quiet at last, sat on a bench watching them. "Isn't this wonderful weather," her mother said.

"I can't believe it's cold and snowy back in Michigan."

"Do you ski?"

"Yes, a little, I'm not terribly good at it."

"Oh, I think you should be. You look so well coordinated."

It was nice plain talk.

Then her mother said, "Sometimes, it still seems like a dream to me that you're here." She stroked Terri's hand. "I think of all that I missed . . . that I'll never get back. Eight years—"

Yes, Terri thought, that's true, no matter how much we talk, that part belongs to Daddy. She looked down at their hands, saw that they were alike. She was beginning to love Kathryn, in a sense had loved her immediately, but this was different, something growing quietly and strongly. Her mother. Her mother.

Twenty-five

"What kind of food do you like, Terri?" my mother asked when I first came. I said, "Oh, anything." It turns out we both love pickles and hate beets. We keep finding out things about ourselves that are alike. We both choose pale green as a favorite color and neither of us can eat an orange first thing in the morning without feeling a little sick to our stomach.

Leah and I are getting to know each other. This morning when I woke up—I'm sleeping on the fold-out couch in her room—she said, "You stayed away so long. We was worried." But she still won't cuddle with me the way Leif does.

It's different living in a house with more people. Something's going on all the time—someone calling to someone else, doors opening and shutting, the radio or TV on, food being fixed—and the phone, that doesn't seem to ever stop ringing. Mom says it usually isn't this bad, but people are calling about us. Yesterday there was an article in the newspaper with a picture of everyone hugging me that first day and crying.

My grandparents came over. They've been coming over every night for supper. Grandmother thought the article was wonderful. She especially liked that she and Grandfather were mentioned. She said it was good for Grandfather's insurance business.

"Ma!" my mother said. "What a thing to say!"

Grandmother said, "Well, it's true, Kathryn. This will get your father's name around more. Look, right here, they tell what he does." She pointed to the place where the article said Grandfather sold insurance and she worked in a doctor's office. "You know what they say, all's fair in love and war."

"Well, your line of reasoning really escapes me!" Mom said. Merle and Grandfather just laughed.

We had Christmas. Food, presents, the tree, eggnog—everything, but it was strange for me. I felt weird all day. Daddy called in the afternoon, and we talked a little bit. That wasn't too good. Maybe I was thinking too much that everyone could hear me.

I've decided I like being in a house with more people. I like that sort of humming feeling of never being alone. But then, somehow, I get so I do want to be alone—at least for a few minutes. This journal helps me be alone. I go off, sit down (I'm in the backyard right now sitting on the edge of Leah's sandbox), and write a little. But every time I go off, it seems that after a bit someone finds me. Merle, or Grandmother, or Leah. "Are you okay, Terri?" "Do you want to go for a walk?" "Are you hungry?" "Want to go for a ride in the car?"

I'm not used to all that attention. Sometimes I like it, and sometimes I think that it doesn't have anything to do with me. Why should everyone be worried so much if I'm happy every second? It makes me feel uncomfortable.

I found out Leah is only two days older than Leif. That is quite a coincidence. She talks more than Leif, is much skinnier, and where he rumbles and bangs into everything, and is sort of like a little heavy-duty truck moving through the world, she twirls and whirls everywhere, more like a <u>leaf</u> than he is! I think she's getting over being so jealous of me.

The kitchen is the gathering place. Everyone seems to end up here, even if it's not time to eat. The telephone is here, and there's a portable TV, and Merle likes to have his "family conferences" here, and Mom says she likes people around when she's cooking. It's Sunday, raining, Grandmother and Grandfather have been here all day. Grandmother started talking about Daddy. "He always was a spoiled boy."

"Now, Ma, really—" Mom made a face. She gave me a bowl of chopped meat and asked me to make the meat patties.

"Well, it's true." Grandmother lit a cigarette. Mom said, "Smoking again?" I thought she wanted to change the subject. So did Grandmother. "Don't change the subject, Kathryn. What is it? You don't want me to talk about Phil in front of Terri? I'm sure it comes as no shock to her. She's an intelligent, smart, bright girl." She patted my hand. "Do you mind that I say that about your father? He was a spoiled boy, you know, spoiled by Vivian. She just doted on him, he could do no wrong was her motto. And I said so from the beginning when you brought him home to meet us, Kathryn."

"Ma, you thought Phil was just great, you liked him a lot."

"Well, he was <u>charming</u>, but I always said he was spoiled."

Grandfather was peeling an avocado for the salad he was making. "Kathryn's right, Ethel. You liked Phil so much you even gave him that watch inscribed with your father's name."

"What watch?" Grandmother said.

Mom and Grandfather both went, <u>"WHAT WATCH?"</u> And I remembered the silver watch inscribed on the back that I found in Daddy's locked

174

box. "Your grandmother likes to rewrite history," Grandfather said to me.

"Does she ever!" Mom said. I felt sort of sorry for Grandmother.

Mom and Leah and I looked at pictures together. There was one of me taken the first day I went to kindergarten, wearing a pleated skirt and looking pretty perky. My resemblance at that age to Leah now is really amazing. I'm sure if anyone looked at that picture and then at Leah, they would know we are sisters.

Leah leaned on me and said, "My mama sleeps with that picture under her pillow. It is her little girl Terri."

"Now I don't anymore, sweetie," Mom said, putting the picture back in the album.

"I know, I know," Leah said. "Because Terri is here." She really is very smart.

Daddy, Barkley, the camper, our apartment—all of it feels so remote to me. Sometimes it's like I've always been here. It's just a week, and that's the way I feel, and it's even a good feeling. Except—what about Daddy? Mom wants me to stay, I mean really stay, live here. She doesn't even want me to go home to get my stuff. "Your father can ship your clothes and things." She and Merle want to fix up the spare room for me. It's not really a room, more sort of an alcove with a window, but it would be big enough for a bed and a bureau, and Merle said he'd get one of his students, who's handy, to build a door. I didn't say no.

Went to the store for Mom. On the way, a kid playing on the street got in front of me. "Where are you going?" He probably wasn't that much older than Leah, but he acted real tough.

"To the market for my mother."

"Who's she?"

"My mother, Mr. Smarty," I said, "is my mother."

"Huh?"

So I said it again. "My mother, Mr. Smarty, is my mother."

Oh, I liked that! My mother is my mother. It made perfect sense to me, and sounded in my head like a piece of music.

In the market I couldn't find the Norwegian sardines Mom wanted. I asked a woman if she knew where the sardines were. "My mother wants them," I said. That was okay, but then I couldn't seem to stop saying, My mother this . . . My mother that . . . "They're my mother's favorite sardines." "My mother only wants that special kind." "My mother loves Norwegian sardines." All the time this poor lady was steering me to the right aisle, she probably thought I was mental. Hearing myself saying <u>My mother</u> gave me this almost scary thrill. As if I was doing something wonderful and forbidden, and I kept wanting to laugh. (At least I got the sardines.)

Something very strange today. I went for a walk with Grandfather after supper. We were just chatting. He told me how he used to be this terrific softball player and how he still loves the game. "We'll have to get up a game one of these weekends," he said. "Let's see, you and me, Grandma, your mother, Merle, that's more than half a team already."

And right then, it came to me that I had been cheated. That for <u>eight years I had been cheated.</u> Cheated of my family, my grandparents, my sister, my mother. And it was Daddy who had cheated me. I had the most hateful, sickening thoughts. That Daddy had lied to me, cheated me, <u>taken me,</u> taken everything away from me. I went completely weak. I leaned against a tree. I was trembling, rubbing my knuckles against the tree.

"Terri!" Grandfather grabbed my hands. "Look

what you're doing to yourself, dear!" I had scraped my knuckles raw. They were bleeding.

Night, under the covers . . . flashlight, Leah sleeping . . . I hear Mom and Merle in the other room. Say to myself, That is my mother in there. I can open the door, call her, and she'll answer, come to see what I want.

This morning, Merle made breakfast. "Everybody out of the kitchen. I'm cooking." A huge feast— southern spoon bread, fried potatoes, ham omelette, fruit salad, and cocoa. While we were eating, Mom said, "Give me your hand, Terri. Hold it up." She put her fingers against mine. "Merle, look, our fingers are the same. Look, we both have long fingers with very short square nails. And look at Terri's thumb—it's just like mine, with that little kink in it."

Holding my hand up against hers, the warmth of her hand against mine, I knew I didn't want to leave.

Twenty-six

"Hello, Daddy?"

"Terri! Terri, honey, how are you?"

"I'm fine, Daddy. How are you?"

"Well, lonely for you, and looking forward to next week when you come home. But, otherwise, okay."

Terri stared out through the phone booth at the school across the street. From the decorations in the window it looked like it was an elementary school. So that wouldn't be the one she'd go to. "How's Barkley?"

"Oh, the old boy misses you, keeps going into your room and whining, and then looking at me, like, 'Hey, mister, what's going on?' "

Terri wet her lips. This wasn't going to be easy. "Well, I called to tell you something."

"What's that, honey?" She felt his voice was sharpened by foreknowledge. "You sound serious."

"I—" She cleared her throat. "Daddy—" Was there a right way to say this? "I want to stay here," she said.

"Stay there?" he repeated.

"Stay. With my mother."

"You mean stay longer?"

"No," she said. "Stay."

"So that's how it is," he said, after a moment. "So that's what happened. So that's what Kathryn has been up to."

"No—it's my decision," she said, gathering breath. "It's my own decision."

178

There was a long silence. The sun struck off the glass booth.

"You and Kathryn are getting along?" he asked abruptly.

"Yes. I like her. I love her," she said humbly, not wanting to hurt him. "I'll come visit you," she said.

"Visit? *Visit?* You know I want more than that!"

Hadn't all this happened before? The sharpness in her throat, the sense of being torn . . . pain like a worm threading its way behind her eyes . . . Yes, she remembered. One of the first phone calls with her mother, standing in the grungy booth outside Azria's . . . and her mother crying, *I want more!* And here she was again in a phone booth, cleaner, indeed sparkling, and the California sun shining as the Michigan sun had not. But no matter, it was all the same. *I want more . . . I want more . . .* They both wanted, her mother and her father, wanted and wanted, and she had to choose.

"It's only fair," she said, her throat tight.

"Fair?"

"You had me for eight years—"

"Yes, and now what, Terri? You call that loyalty? I thought I brought you up better than that."

"Daddy!" She couldn't keep the pain and anger out of her voice. "You're unfair."

"I want you to come home—Terri—"

"Unfair!" She wouldn't let him talk, soothe her, persuade her. "Can't you leave me alone!" And she hung up on him.

That night she had a dream. Apparently, it was California, her mother's house, but it was a big room, empty except for two chairs. Her father was sitting in one chair. The other was empty. She saw that her father was defeated, and it hurt her, but at the same time, because he had taken so much from her, it made her glad. He deserved to be defeated and hurt. She stared at him hard, giving him a proud look, not letting his humble, defeated eyes make her turn away.

"You had it all your way for so long," she said.

179

"You had it your way for eight years." It was like a song. *You had it your way* . . . It was good that he was hurting. He would hurt for a little while or for a long time, but in any case it would never make up for what he had stolen from her mother and her.

But all the time she thought this she noticed the way he sat very straight and kept a little smile in the corners of his mouth, as if he were determined not to give in to the defeat, determined not to break down. And this pleased her. She thought, My father is a fighter, he won't give up. She was pleased with him for not crying, for not begging, and at the same time she felt such an astonishing wave of pity for him that she understood that she must love him very much. Despite everything, she still loved him very, very much.

Two days later, she received a letter from Nancy.

Dear Terri,
    I wanted you to hear this from me.
Last night Phil and I had a long
talk, and the upshot was that we
are breaking off our relationship.
It will not be mended again. I'll
be frank with you--I am the one
who wants this, not Phil. I'm not
happy about it, but I don't see
what else to do, Terri. No new
reasons, really, only more of the
same things that you and I talked
about.
    Phil can't, or won't, understand
or admit that what he did when he
took you was WRONG. We have talked
about it from every angle and we are
too far apart in our beliefs and
views.
    I still love him, but with such a
profound sense of doubt, such

180

bewilderment, that it no longer
means happiness for me to be with
him. I guess you know I hoped that
someday we would get married. But
how could I marry and have his
child (which I would want) and <u>not</u>
live in fear that if our marriage
didn't work, he would take our
child and run, <u>as he did with you?</u>

Dear Terri, this was happening
before you left. I didn't want to
put a cloud over your trip. But
now it's all come to an end. I love
you very much. Do you know how
much I wish that things could have
worked out? But it isn't meant to
be. Much love,
Nancy.
P.S. Leif loved his letter from
you. So did I!

Twenty-seven

"I wonder if the mailman has come yet?" Merle said, looking out the side window. They were sitting around the counter in the kitchen eating a banana cream pie that Ethel and Bob had brought over. "Want to get the mail, Leah?"

"Yeah!" Leah bent to hastily pull on her blue ballet slippers. The rest of her outfit was a pair of blue underpants and a sleeveless tee shirt.

"One of these days you'll send Leah for the mail and you'll be sorry," Kathryn said. Wearing a high-necked green shirt, jeans, and a green cotton scarf tied bandit fashion around her forehead, she looked especially splendid to Terri. "There'll be a thousand-dollar check in the mail and—"

Merle tipped back in his chair. "Where would that thousand dollars come from?"

"Some mysterious rich relative we've forgotten, who remembers us." She took another slice of pie. "I've got to stop eating this. Ma, you shouldn't bring rich stuff like this around."

"Oh, what's life without a little cream pie on New Year's Day," Terri's grandfather said. "Right, Terri?"

"Right, Grandfather." Outside it was raining again, a dismal greyish day. Inside, the overhead light with its red Chinese lantern shade cast a warm glow over the counter. Terri was wearing jeans and a pale lime green shirt (same color as her mother's), but everyone else was more brilliant: her grandmother in a bright yellow dress with an orange and yellow bow at her neck, her grandfather in his pink cowboy shirt with the pearl buttons, and even Merle had added red suspenders to hold up his plaid pants.

"Two more days and school starts," he said, rocking in his chair, arms folded on his chest. "And Terri and I will be going together. Now that's going to be nice!"

They all looked at her, their smiles like a warm bath.

"Wait till the boys see her," her grandfather said. "All those California beauties will have to move over."

"Grandfather!" Terri smiled, but felt a twinge of alarm. All morning she had been feeling let down and uneasy; she didn't know why, and that made her especially quiet. It couldn't be the prospect of the new school; she'd gone through all that too often.

The night before, New Year's Eve, they had celebrated with a big dinner—bowls of food and plenty of wine. Long before midnight, her mother had cried, kissing Terri and pulling her down on her lap. With her mother's arms tightly around her waist, Terri had leaned back and drifted into one of those exquisite and unspeakable moments of happiness. Then, seeing Leah, face flushed, she had pulled her sister onto *her* lap.

"It's a sandwich," Leah had said.

Amidst the laughter, Merle had gone scurrying for his camera. "I gotta have that shot for the family album!"

As much as she had felt part of and inside the bright warmth of her family circle last night, Terri now felt herself separated, drifting on the outside. It was so bad to feel this way . . . to feel something nagging, almost sore . . . and a kind of greyness, like a veil between herself and everyone else. Her eyes went out of focus. The worst part was not knowing why she felt like this.

Leah came in. "I got the letters." Her hands were behind her back.

"Give them to Mommy," Kathryn said.

"No. I'll open the letters." Her eyes sparkled with mischief.

"Leah—"

"Give them to Gramma, sweetie."

"No."

"Leah . . ."

"No."

"Now, Leah, little girl, listen to Grampy—"

She was delighted with the attention; her eyes swept from one adult to the other, lighting at last on her sister. "I'll give the letters to Terri," she decided. "Okay? Okay?"

"Don't agree with her," Kathryn said, "or she'll change her mind. Leah, I think you have all the makings of a power broker."

"A definite lust for power," Merle agreed. Leah went to Terri.

Her hands came from behind her back.

"No mail!" she said.

"No mail?" Merle said.

"I tricked you," Leah said.

"Oh, what's the matter with us anyway?" Kathryn said. "It's New Year's Day—no mail today."

Shifting in her seat, Terri felt Nancy's letter folded in her back pocket and thought of the letter she had tried to write her father. She had wanted to tell him that she knew about Nancy, that she was sorry and was thinking of him. It had all come out sounding mealy-mouthed and phoney-sweet.

"Is something the matter?" her mother asked, leaning toward her. Terri shook her head. "You're so quiet, honey." She tied her pirate scarf tighter at the back of her head.

"No, I'm fine."

"Okay . . ." Her mother put her hand over Terri's, and Terri had an impulse to kiss her mother's hand, but she didn't. She felt a dislike for herself, a surge of dissatisfaction that made her reach for another slice of cream pie. She stuffed in the sweetness and felt worse.

And then, finally, looking around at the family, listening to the bickering and bantering, she thought about her father. What was *he* doing now? Who was *he* with? No one, she answered herself with cold clarity.

And she saw a vivid picture of him at home in the living room, maybe eating a cheese sandwich, Barkley lying on the floor, and the TV on to the Rose Bowl. And that was it . . .

This image so upset her that she couldn't sit there another moment. She left the table and got a jacket.

"Where're you going?" her mother said.

"Out for a walk."

"I'll go with you," Leah offered.

"No, Leah, it's raining," Kathryn said.

"Terri's going!"

"Yes, but she's a big girl."

"I am, too!"

"Terri," Merle said, "see if you can find a drugstore that's open and buy us shampoo, okay?"

"Any special kind?" she asked.

"Anything you like. Here—" He gave her some money.

"Come back soon, sweetie," her grandmother said. "Wait, wait, let me kiss you." She pulled Terri's head down and smacked her heartily on both cheeks.

"Ma, she's just going for a walk."

"I want to go, too," Leah said.

"That's all right, maybe it's just a walk to you," her grandmother said, "but to me, I still want to kiss her every time she goes out of my sight."

"Ethel's emotional," her grandfather said, brushing back his hair.

"I'll see you all pretty soon," Terri said. Outside, she drew in a deep breath of the cool wet air. She walked for a long time. Why were things in life so unfair? Why couldn't everyone be happy at the same time? Why was it that if you thought of one person, you probably hurt the other person? Why couldn't someone come along and make things right—Wonder

185

Woman, or Superman, she wouldn't care! Just someone who could say, Terri, do *this* and do *that* and you can have what you want, and they'll *all* feel good.

Because what she wanted was her mother. And what she wanted was her father. And what she didn't want was to do what she had done—to choose one over the other.

And thinking this, walking through the rain, she thought how for years her mother had nothing . . . *nothing* . . . while her father had her, and then her and Nancy and Leif. Now her mother had Merle, Grandmother and Grandfather, Leah, and Terri . . . and her father had nothing . . . *nothing*.

Her head was wet. She kept walking.

When she came back, they had all moved into the living room. Her grandparents were lying on the couch next to each other, asleep. The TV was on, her mother was reading, and Leah was curled in Merle's lap, sucking her thumb. A bowl of fruit was on the coffee table.

"Mom," Terri said, "can I talk to you?"

Her mother put down her magazine. "Private?"

Terri nodded. They went into her mother's room and closed the door. "You're soaked," her mother said, taking a towel from a wicker laundry basket in the corner and toweling Terri's hair.

"Mom," Terri said, her head bent beneath her mother's hands, "I have to change my mind. I've got to go back."

Her mother's hands went on toweling her head. Maybe the words had been muffled. Kathryn seemed to have heard only "change," and asked, "Are your feet wet, too?"

"Mom." Terri put her hands over her mother's and looked up. "I have to go back to Daddy. I have to." The words seemed awful and full of the truth.

"Why?" her mother said.

"He has nothing now . . . and I love him . . . and I feel sorry for him."

Now her mother heard her. "Sorry? Did he feel sorry

186

for me when I was alone? Alone, Terri? He doesn't know what the word means. *I* was alone," she said passionately. "I was alone for four years until I met Merle. I was alone without you for eight years. Let me tell you something, Terri! If I had my way, Phil would be alone forever, because alone is hell, and I think he deserves it."

"No, he doesn't." Terri's voice was choked. "I don't even—I can't talk to you about this—"

"So it's not settled," her mother said. "Will it ever be settled? I don't want you to go!" Her voice rose. And roughly she went on toweling Terri's head.

Terri was near tears. She thought of the little toy that her grandfather had brought for Leah, the old-fashioned wooden toy with a little green monkey, arms outstretched, dangling between two bars. When you squeezed the bottom of the bars together, the monkey flipped over. When you didn't squeeze, there the monkey dangled, arms stretched wide between the bars. And that was how she felt—the monkey on the bars. The monkey in the middle.

"Eight years," her mother said. "Eight years."

The tears broke. "No. No . . . please." Terri stood there, not moving, tears sliding down her face.

"Oh, my dear," her mother said. "Oh, my dear. Don't cry, don't cry." She blotted Terri's tears with the towel. "No, *don't* let me make you cry."

Then they held each other as they had at the airport. "I know you have to do this," her mother said. "I know you're doing what you feel is right. I know it. You mustn't listen to me—I let my anger speak. I love you." She kissed Terri's face repeatedly. "I love you, and I'm not going to lose you again. And I'll tell you something else," she said. "I know how hard it is for you. And I'm proud of you. I'm so proud of you. I wouldn't want you any other way than the way you are. I love you, I love you."

"And I love you," Terri said.

Twenty-eight

Dear dearest Mother,
  I'm writing this in study hall.
I wanted to write you lots sooner,
but it seemed like there was a lot
to do every single day this week.
All the teachers load us up with
work in the new term, I guess.
Anyway, from now on, I really will
write you every week just the way
I promised.
  You should have seen Barkley when
I came home. He went wild. He was
really happy to see me. I was
pretty happy to see him, too!
  I know that you and I talked
everything over, but I still want
to say something. I don't want you
to be hurt by what I did--I mean,
coming back to live with Daddy. I
don't want you to ever think that
I did it because there was anything
wrong with living with you.
  I love you and Leah, and everyone
else, but I love Daddy, too, and I
can't stop loving him. I know what
he did was wrong. I know it made
people suffer. I know now how much

I lost because of it. But I don't
hate him for it. I can't and I
never will.
   I will come to live with you over
the summer the way we talked about
it. And I hope very much that
Daddy will agree to move to
California so that I can see you
often.
   Dearest Mother, I love you with
all my heart, and I miss you very
very much.

Your daughter always,
Terri.

A Note To Our Readers

If in reading TAKING TERRI MUELLER, you think that Terri's story may be your story, and that there may be a parent looking for you, then you should know about CHILD FIND.
CHILD FIND is the center point for missing children and their searching parents. CHILD FIND helps parents and children find one another. For more information contact:

CHILD FIND, INC.
P.O. Box 277
New Paltz, New York 12561
1-800-431-5005

If you are a child in New York State call:

1-914-255-1848 collect

NORMA FOX MAZER grew up in Glens Falls, New York, in the foothills of the Adirondack Mountains. She has been writing all her life and is the author of seven acclaimed books for young readers. Ms. Mazer currently makes her home in Central New York State with her husband and the youngest of their four children.

When asked why she wrote TAKING TERRI MUELLER, Ms. Mazer replied, "I read that there are an estimated 25,000 children stolen each year in the aftermath of divorce and that most of them will never see their mothers again. I was not only saddened by this bleak statistic, I was also startled and fascinated that in the name of love adults would deprive their children not only of a parent but of family and friends, community and stability. I wrote this book for both adults and children. First, because it's a story I think everyone can connect to; and second—as in all my writing for young people—to say, 'Okay, life is not easy, but don't despair. There is strength inside you.'"